TASTING HER

TASTING HER

ORAL SEX STORIES

Edited by
Rachel Kramer Bussel

Cleis Press Inc., P.O. Box 14697, San Francisco, California 94114
Printed in the United States.

Cover design: Scott Idleman
Cover photograph: April/Getty Images
Text design: Frank Wiedemann
Cleis logo art: Juana Alicia
First Edition.
10 9 8 7 6 5 4 3

Contents

INTRODUCTION: READING HER LIPS

Whether you've delved between a woman's legs, received cunnilingus, or fantasized about either, *Tasting Her* has a lot to offer you. To be honest, I'm usually not the biggest fan, personally, of getting head. Often it feels either rushed or perfunctory, or like I'm not sure how long I should give the person until we move on to something else. I don't always know when or how I will come, though plenty of women swear by a little tongue-lashing (or a lot!) to do the trick.

What's great about this collection is that there are oral sex connoisseurs and newcomers, men and women who explore the treasure to be found in a woman's pussy, often in surprising ways. Maybe they think they know everything there is to know about giving (and getting) head, but have a partner who wants to show them something new.

We sometimes forget, given stories about men who refuse to go there (and yes, I've encountered a few), that there are plenty of men and women who truly enjoy, relish, and get turned on by basking in a woman's sex. The kind who find eating pussy not just a pit stop on the way to something greater, but the ultimate pleasure. Sometimes this can take the form of a BDSM scene, where someone is being "forced" to do what he really loves best. At other times, these happy lickers have to convince their partners that they want it so bad they'll do anything to get it.

In Jen Cross's outstanding story, "Queen of Sheba," we meet one such couple:

Jimmy would use his hands to hold me open, and his whole mouth, his nose and chin and cheeks. He'd fuck me with his tongue, then lap at me with the full flat of it, wriggle the tip across my clit, then capture the fat little head between his thin lips and suckle first gently, then more sharply, as I came. And came. And came.

He got me off so many times when he was down there, like that was the whole point. Can you imagine?

Her narrator learns that some men treat a woman's pussy like it's the pinnacle of her body, even when the woman herself may be a little puzzled as to what he loves about it so much.

I've been in the position of Gwen Masters's Teresa in "Teaching Teresa," refusing to let someone go down on me simply because I didn't think it would be all that fun. The last person I tried that with, though, used my refusal as a pawn in our sexual game, and when I let him advance, he showed me just how wonderful a well-placed tongue could feel. I think he wanted to show me what I'd been missing. In Masters's story, our hero has to articulate what it is he enjoys about the act:

"I love everything about it," he told her. "I love the smell—that deep and secret scent. I love the taste. I love the way it changes

when a woman comes, and the way it changes again after I've been inside her. It's like I can taste all the different levels of arousal."

Teresa was looking up at him with wide eyes.

"Most of all, I love the way a woman moves. I love the way the same touches can get a different reaction every time. But I also love finding that one thing that drives a woman crazy every time."

Other lessons are imparted throughout this collection, and I can tell you that by the end of the editing process, I was more than ready to spread my legs. Whatever your feelings about going down, I hope this book will broaden your horizons, and expose you to the ways cunnilingus can become part of a relationship, a quickie fling, a BDSM scene, and so much more. The characters here, from the dedication of the man who gives geographical names to specific parts of his lover's sexual anatomy in Jeremy Edwards's "Cavanuagh's Ridge" to the kinky pleasures of the couple in Teresa Noelle Roberts's "The Dominance of the Tongue," have a thing or two to teach you about pussy power. Savor them and their adventures, as well as your own.

Rachel Kramer Bussel
New York City

CAVANAUGH'S RIDGE

Jeremy Edwards

Estelle was so tense, she was ticklish. I don't mean "hee hee, do that again" ticklish; I mean so ticklish that if I kissed her between the legs, she'd leap three feet in the air—from a horizontal position, mind you.

So it had been weeks since I'd kissed her between the legs.

Oh, we had sex. Good sex. I was a creative guy, and there were a lot of things I could find to do that didn't involve kissing Estelle between her luscious thighs. I did them all. And she did things, too. She may have been tense as a guitar string, but she knew how to get both of us off.

But my face missed her pussy, the intimacy of my lips on her most personal flesh, right there; the delicate flavor, so elegant and yet so animal, the perfect essence of beauty in heat. And I missed getting a full nose of the accompanying aroma—because if I'd stuck my nose in there, she would have jumped *four* feet.

Sometimes I would lie there at night after coming heavily into her, after pumping and grinding her into her own tense little orgasms…and I would imagine her pussy in my face. It became an obsession, a pot of gold at the end of a rainbow. Yes, I'd been inside her moments earlier, but now I dreamed of making love to her all over again with my lips, of tasting her on my tongue.

I could visualize Estelle's pussy in complete, meticulous detail—just as I could visualize the topographical map of our county if I shut my eyes (and had nothing better to visualize). No two landscapes look alike, and I had studied every valley, slope, swirl, and crevice of the private national park between Estelle's legs. As I lay there at night imagining her map spread out for me, I felt like a horny park ranger, giving myself a tour.

I even invented names for some of the geographical features of Estelle's vulva. There was one lovely fold at the left that I dubbed "Cavanaugh's Ridge." I had no idea where I got that—I'd never known anybody named Cavanaugh—but it just sounded right. It sounded right in my head, to be more precise. I didn't actually tell Estelle that I'd embellished her genitals, in my mind, with cartographic nomenclature. I was afraid that might make her tense.

Eventually, I figured out how to get my lips as close as I could to Estelle's snatch, without setting off her tickle alarm. To be specific, I learned that I could kiss her on the knee without it bothering her. On the front of the knee or the outside edge, that is. Not on the inside—and definitely not around back, behind the joint. No way.

Why was Estelle so tense? There was no overriding reason. But there were a lot of little reasons. Estelle was tense because two of her coworkers had resigned, and she was picking up the slack. She was tense because her mother was getting married and felt obligated to consult Estelle about every fucking detail regarding the wedding plans—though she never, ultimately, paid attention to any of poor Estelle's suggestions. She was tense because she'd committed to training for a 10k with her buddies, but she kept standing them up for runs because of the situation at work.

Nothing serious, nothing that wouldn't fix itself...but in the meantime, Estelle was tense.

We had strategies. The self-hypnosis made her a little more mentally placid, but I still couldn't get near her delicious juncture with my lips. The wine put her to sleep. That was good, insofar as she could use some extra z's—but it did not address the issue at hand.

I suggested massage, but Estelle gently reminded me that she didn't have the patience to lie still for that sort of thing. I might as well suggest she take a goddamn thirty-minute *bath*, she told me.

Estelle was as discouraged as I was. She missed my mouth down there.

Then I realized we were approaching this from the wrong direction. We'd been assuming that the first step was to relax her, and that this would then open up a route to Cavanaugh's Ridge and environs. It finally occurred to me that the road to success didn't just end with my mouth on her body—it began there.

"Lie as still as you can," I quietly advised, on the night we'd set aside. "Don't worry about relaxing, because that might make you *un*relaxed. Just lie there, and let me worry about everything."

I found the spot on her left kneecap that represented, in my experience, the northernmost place, below the waist, that I could kiss her these days without her squirming in an unsexy fashion.

I kissed her there—not too softly, not too intensely. Solidly.

"How does that feel?"

"Nice," she said pleasantly, if not exactly passionately.

I did it again. And again. I knew I had to kiss her kneecap till the sensation became so predictable to her that it was downright boring.

"How you doing?" I asked, after a few dozen knee kisses.

"Okay."

"Getting a little bored?"

"Well, you know..." She was too kind to actually say it.

"I'm going to try something different now." And I did: I began kissing her *right* kneecap, in the same manner.

"Randolph..."

"*Shh*," I urged soothingly, resisting the impulse to say that counterproductive word, *relax*.

Truth be told, it wasn't that boring on my end. Maybe I was imagining things, but I could swear that Estelle's right knee tasted different from her left knee. They were both savory—fresh and feminine and familiar—but the right knee seemed a smidgen saltier, where the left was slightly sweeter.

But this wasn't about knee-to-knee recipe tests. This was about kissing Estelle at the edge of her safe zone until she was so used to the feeling—so totally, tediously accustomed to it—that her nervous system's irrational defenses would flag, and her skin would welcome my mouth's ascent like in the old days. That was the theory, anyhow.

Finally, I could tell that if I kissed her knee one more time, she would be likely to sit up and start doing a crossword puzzle.

"Hey," I said, softly.

"Hey."

I positioned my lips about a centimeter farther up her leg, just enough to cross from knee territory to thigh jurisdiction, in the eyes of an anatomy specialist. Then I gave her the lightest possible kiss, and I braced myself for the dreaded feeling of Estelle tensing up and shivering.

She didn't. She didn't do anything, in fact. I wondered if my kiss had been so light that she hadn't even felt it. Maybe it didn't count.

"That feels good," she said quietly.

Those three words made me want to cry with hope. But I knew I still had a long way to go, and I had to keep both my calm and my momentum. So I tried not to think too much, and I focused on kissing her thigh again—just as lightly, but another centimeter higher.

Again, I waited for a reaction—I was prepared now for either a positive one or a negative one—but all I perceived was Estelle's regular breathing. That was good, though.

And so I went higher still. Emboldened, I advanced up her thigh without waiting to see how she would react to each and every touch of my lips. I trusted in the inevitability of my progress and the regularity of my rhythm to keep her body from freaking out. I trusted in my knowledge that, despite the obstructive behavior of her nerves in recent weeks, Estelle wanted this as badly as I did.

On some level, I still couldn't believe it. I was kissing Estelle's sweet upper thigh, and nothing bad was happening. She was even purring a bit now.

But I knew the proof was in the pudding, and I hadn't yet gone near her pudding. With that dessert in mind, I took two bold steps, in conjunction with each other: I shifted my focus to the *inside* surface of her thigh, and I introduced my tongue into the equation.

I licked her flesh with a slow, even pressure. I wanted to ensure that it was a caress and not a tickle. Someday, I knew, little tickle games could once again be a part of our love life. At the moment, however, *tickle* was a dirty word.

When I found that I was painting Estelle's inner thigh with

my tongue and she was, believe it or not, relaxing into it, I became incredibly hard. Up until this point, I'd been treating this encounter as a sort of experiment, and my commitment to it, though emotionally impassioned, had not been notably sexual. Now, with her body beginning to melt for me and the first wafts of her arousal luring me closer to her pussy, my cock was waking up—and making up for lost time.

As I slowly, carefully kissed and licked my way up her thigh, I kept my eye on the pot of gold. There it shone, in all its natural beauty: the majestic clitoris that I'd nicknamed "Pleasure Rock"; the sculpted region at the base of her opening, where her wetness had a tendency to pool—as it was doing now—and which, on my mental map, was labeled "Slick Shallows"; and, of course, Cavanaugh's Ridge.

It was all I could do to resist rushing in there, drooling and smooching and tonguing her like a wild beast. But the high I was getting from knowing how far we'd come gave me the self-control to maintain the pace. So I inched my way up, cautiously but unhesitatingly, and I listened to the intense—but reassuringly serene—moans from Estelle.

When, at last, I arrived home, I wasn't sure whether to start with my tongue or my lips. But she made that decision for me.

"Lick me," she whispered.

So I licked her—first, around the periphery, the very outer edges of her sex, which had remained largely dry, though moisture was trickling earnestly from her cavity down onto the mattress.

Then, when I was pretty sure the market would bear it, I moved my tongue down to the Slick Shallows and began to lick upward—straight up and down the center of her slit this time, right where she was weeping shimmering fluid.

Her folds tasted even more succulent than I'd remembered,

and as she squirmed—erotically, thank goodness, not hyper-sensitively—I felt her pussy licking me back. I kissed her cunt now, repeatedly, the way I'd kissed her face at the train station a couple of months earlier, after we'd had to spend a week apart. Next, I let my tongue penetrate her, and I danced it inside her while listening to her gasp—sensuously, not nervously.

Then, while holding firmly on to her knees, I licked Pleasure Rock. Once. Twice. Three times.

And Estelle came for me, shuddering and wailing as if she were releasing every last drop of tension that had been trapped inside her for so long. She came for me and, most important, for herself, as if a thousand little corked vials of stress had opened all at once and were spilling out from between her legs.

I kept licking her while she came, until she was so trans-ported by ecstasy and relief that my tongue became superfluous to her experience. At that point, I pulled my face back—still holding her knees—to see her pulses of pleasure throb across her beautiful vulval landscape.

And I watched Cavanaugh's Ridge twitch like my own dancing cock, which now spurted dollop after dollop of grati-tude onto Estelle's right ankle.

SNATCH

Donna George Storey

We were just getting ready to do it when Eliot's boss called. I could tell it was Roger by the ring tone: Darth Vadar's theme song.

Eliot paused, one hand on my breast, the other between my legs. "Shit. I'm sorry, Brianna. I told him he could call after eleven if there was a problem with the new build."

He reached over me to pick up his cell, apparently oblivious that his fingers were slick with my juices. I pressed my cheek into the pillow to hide my disappointment. We'd already had sex once this morning—great sex—and it didn't seem wise to come across as an insatiable nympho so early in a promising relationship.

"Yeah, okay. I can come in to the office. No problem." He hung up, then looked over at me, his handsome face crumpled in apology. "I feel awful about this, especially since it's Saturday. But those bozos can't seem to do a thing without me."

"That's okay. I have some stuff to do at home anyway."

"Could you stay? I'll have them on track in less than an hour. And I'll make it up to you when I get back. I'll lick your delicious pussy for hours until you come ten times."

I laughed at his boast, but actually, given Eliot's skill with his tongue, it was more of a guarantee.

"I guess I could stay. Can I check my email while I'm waiting?"

"Absolutely. My laptop's in the dining room. I'll log you in before I go."

As for what happened next, well, in my defense, I started out fully intending to be a polite guest and a trustworthy girlfriend. It was actually Eliot's fault for having his browsing history open, irresistibly, in the upper corner of the screen. There, beneath the websites I'd visited—Gmail, Facebook, and Amazon—glittered a column of intriguing folder icons marked *Yesterday, Two Days Ago*...all the way down to *One Week Ago*.

Which was, in fact, the very day Eliot had whispered that he thought he was falling in love with me. Unfortunately, he told me this as we were basking in the afterglow of another round of sizzling copulation. And I'd heard that line too often in exactly the same circumstances. When you moan and squirm in bed like I do, guys tend toward a premature ejaculation of the *L* word when they really just mean they like the sex. So I laughed—a warm, encouraging laugh because I liked Eliot a lot—and asked how he could love me if he didn't really know me yet. "I want to know everything about you," he replied. It was probably then that I started falling a little bit in love myself.

This meant, of course, that I wanted to know everything about him, too. Such as, for example, where he'd been surfing the Internet four days ago, when we'd spent the night apart.

Before my conscience could weigh in with any principled protests, I'd already clicked on the folder, my eyes racing down the column. Foreign Cinema? Eliot had been trying to get us a reservation there—very sweet of him. ESPN? Raidernews.com? He was a Raiders fan even though they'd sucked for years—but I liked loyalty in a man. Christina After Hours? That one stopped me for a moment. Amber Bares All? I was starting to catch on. Shaved Snatch? My chest tightened.

I could easily guess what kind of images my wonderful new boyfriend had been drooling over as he wanked his weenie on Tuesday night. There was no need to click on the link at all.

I did anyway.

I braced myself for the worst as the site loaded onto the screen. Garish close-ups of female genitals with Brazilian wax jobs, trashy-looking blondes grimacing in ersatz ecstasy. Sometimes it was possible to know *too* much about a person. One glance at this sleazy stuff and I'd lose all respect for Eliot, even though he was the nicest guy and the best fuck I'd met in quite some time. But there was no turning back now.

Because suddenly there it was before me: Shaved Snatch in all its glory.

I let out a bark of a laugh. The site was nothing but a list of links to other porn sites. New for This Month: Brunette Shows Off Her Shaved Slit. Pigtailed Teen Dildos Tight Trimmed Pussy.

There was a kind of skanky poetry to it, but I was sharp enough to figure out it was merely the gateway to the evening's real entertainment. Amber Bares All was more what I was expecting: an amateurish photo gallery of a dark-haired "coed" in a cheerleader outfit, stripping off her sweater to show off perky breasts, lifting her skirt to reveal her bald mons. For the grand finale, she fingered herself, glaring into the camera with the stupidest expression I'd ever seen.

I realized, with a pang, that Amber actually looked a lot like me. Except for the stupid expression. Still, I should be flattered, right?

By now the adrenaline had kicked in, and I felt just the barest twinge of guilt as I clicked on Christina's site. Eliot had presumably gone for the tissues while appreciating her clean-shaven charms, if not her requisite goofy come-on look.

Again he surprised me. Instead of cheesy snapshots taken in someone's badly-decorated living room, Christina's show was a classy production: black-and-white film, soft focus. A pretty platinum blonde in nothing but a policeman's cap and leather jacket lounged against some fluffy cushions, gazing down at her splayed, smooth labia with whimsical self-reflection. Next came a close-up of her backside, the pussy lips pouting below her ass cleft—perfectly smooth, swollen, touchable.

I had to admit he showed good taste in masturbation materials with this one. I also had to admit I was getting sort of, well, turned on. Hell, that "take me from behind now" picture even made *me* want to fuck her.

My musings were rudely interrupted by the trill of my cell phone. I jumped guiltily and reached for my purse to answer it.

"Hey, Brianna, it's me. This is going to take longer than I thought. I am so sorry. You're probably really pissed at me."

"Oh, no, I understand," I said sweetly. My own lapse in good behavior had put me in a forgiving mood.

"Listen, a reservation has opened up at Foreign Cinema at seven. Will you meet me down at work this evening?"

"Sure. It sounds like fun. Besides, it turns out I have something important to do on my own this afternoon anyway."

It wasn't a lie either. As soon as we hung up, I deleted the most recent entries—my entries—from the history and logged out. Then I went into Eliot's bathroom where I'd left my travel kit.

My hand trembling slightly, I unzipped the bag and pulled out my razor.

I knew my shaving project would have its dangers. Razor nicks or careless slips of the hand, for example. But I had no idea a bare pussy would be a driving hazard. I didn't figure that out until I was sitting in my car with no underwear on, my secret flesh tingling at the new sensations. *God, I'm so turned on, is this leaving a wet spot on my clothes? What will Eliot do when he sees me? Will he guess where I got the idea? Call me a lousy snoop and kick me out on my bald booty?* So many crazy thoughts were swirling through my mind, I almost sailed straight through two red lights.

The truth was I'd been highly aroused for hours, from the moment I put that razor to my lathered-up mons. I was used to doing my bikini line, but it was very different to shave it all off, each stroke revealing a new strip of satiny white skin, and finally, my tender, pink cleft. Then I had to spread my legs wide to tidy up the labia, which were already swollen and tingly from all the action I'd been getting with Eliot. I couldn't help gazing down at myself, so totally naked and exposed, until I realized, with a pang of guilt, that I was copying Christina's pose exactly.

It took all my self-control not to masturbate, but I figured it'd be worth it to save myself for the man who'd inspired me.

Eliot met me at the door of his office building with a big smile and a hungry kiss. "Come upstairs with me for a minute. I have one quick thing to do before we go to the restaurant. Then I'm your love slave for the rest of the weekend."

I rolled my eyes but was secretly pleased. I had something to do before we went to the restaurant, too.

I lounged on the extra chair in his office, twirling around in circles like a kid. Did he notice I wasn't wearing pantyhose? Could he smell me—the spicy, fresh-bread scent of a horny female without any underpants on?

In fact, he did stop typing at his computer and smile. "You look especially beautiful right now."

"You're just suffering from sex deprivation."

He laughed. "So did you have a good afternoon on your own?"

"I wouldn't necessarily call it 'good.' To be honest, I did something rather...naughty. I hope you're not mad when you find out what it is." I gave him a flirty sidelong look, which, it struck me then, was probably a lot like Amber's idiotic expression.

"I won't mind." His eyes twinkled. "As long as you tell me all about it. In detail."

"I think it's better to show you."

Eliot's eyebrows shot up and he glanced toward the door, although, in fact the building did seem otherwise dark and deserted.

"It probably is a good idea to close the door. And lock it," I added.

I could see it all in his face—the inner struggle between proper etiquette in the workplace and raw sexual curiosity. The next thing I knew, he was standing, easing the door closed, turning the lock button in the knob. Obviously his thirst for knowledge had won out over good manners. I admired that in a person.

I stood and faced him like a gunslinger in a Western. It was time for the Shaved Pussy Showdown. Hiking my skirt up, inch by teasing inch, I watched his jaw drop.

The silence in the room was thick enough to slice with a razor blade.

"What's the matter? You don't like the new me?"

Eliot let out a sound—half sigh, half moan—that made me think he'd forgotten to breathe for quite some time. "Yes, I mean, no, I mean...wow."

I dropped my skirt with feigned nonchalance. "So, now you know what I did this afternoon. I guess we'd better leave now if we want to make that reservation."

"No, not yet, please." Eliot hurried over and fell to his knees before me. "May I...touch it?"

He'd asked so nicely, what could I do but nod and lift my skirt again?

Slowly, reverently, he reached up to trace the exposed groove of my flesh with his fingertip.

Now I was the one having trouble breathing. The whole scene suddenly seemed so strange. Eliot kneeling before me as if in worship, my own lower regions as smooth and white as marble. It was just like some ancient fertility ritual except I wasn't a stone goddess. I was flesh and blood, my pulse throbbing deep inside my belly like a voice. *Touch it again.*

As if in a trance, Eliot nudged me back onto the chair and parted my thighs. He swallowed loudly. Drool. "May I... taste it?"

My face was on fire and my throat so tight, I could barely croak out the words. "Yes...please."

At the first touch of his tongue, I almost leaped out of the chair. I clenched my teeth to stifle a moan. If someone else were still in the building, my cries might send him running to aid a female in distress. But with Eliot lapping me right where the pale white of my outer lips deepened to a dusky rose, I wasn't exactly in distress. It was more like heaven. Yet suddenly I wanted more from him than sensation.

"Eliot?" I whispered. "Do you like it?"

He pulled away, lips glistening. "What do you think?"

I was glad he approved of at least part of my afternoon's activities, but I needed still more. I *did* want to know everything about him. "Why do you like it?"

"Why?" He smiled. "I guess I like licking smooth things. It's like ice cream, but warm. And sweeter."

"You like looking at it, too, don't you?"

His eyes fell to my pussy, spread wide before him. Brunette Shows Her Shaved Slit. Except this time it was real. "Yeah. It's so pink and beautiful, it's like..." He faltered into awed silence.

I almost blew it then and finished for him, "...like the girls on the Internet. Amber and Christina."

Fortunately he was back to lapping my parts again and all that came from my lips was a whimper. He was doing all his usual tricks. Flicking my clit lightly. Making little circles around it with the tip of his tongue. But even with a dedicated muff diver like Eliot, it usually takes me a little while to get into the zone. This time my thighs were shaking and my ass was slipping around on the chair like skates on a frozen pond within moments flat. Everything was so exquisitely sensitive down there, as if my razor had stripped each nerve bare as well. I was teetering on the verge of a bone-crushing car wreck of an orgasm, when Eliot pulled away again.

"Do *you* like it?" he asked.

"What do you think?"

He started stroking me again, circling and teasing, not just the pink parts, but the swollen and silky outer lips. "You seem turned on all right. By the way, how'd you get the idea to do this anyway?"

My secret muscles clenched and fluttered, lust tinged with guilt. "El, I'd love to chat, but if you keep touching me like that I'm gonna come," I panted, clutching the edge of the chair, "and I'd rather do it with your tongue on my clit and two of those long, thick fingers shoved inside."

I wasn't exactly lying, but my request had just the effect I was hoping for—Eliot stopped asking tricky questions and put his tongue right back where I wanted it. He dutifully pushed two fingers inside me with a soft slurp and pressed up against my G-spot, just the way I like it.

With that sweet pressure on my insides and that hot swirling tongue outside, it took only two licks, maybe three, and suddenly I was sailing straight through every red light on the planet, then lifting off, up, up into the sky. I tried to be quiet, but I was thrashing and shaking so much as I came on his mouth, I couldn't restrain a long, guttural moan.

Fortunately, there were no knocks at the door to disturb us—*Watcha doing in there, Eliot, strangling a wild animal?*—as my very hot, very wet boyfriend pulled me down to the floor and took me in his arms. We kissed and I sucked my juices from his lips greedily. He was right. I did taste sweet.

"Brianna? Can I ask you a question? Be honest with me." Eliot's face was suddenly grave.

I braced myself for the real Shaved Snatch Showdown. This time it would be harder to wiggle out of an explanation.

"I know it's almost impossible to get reservations on Saturday," he continued, "but do you mind if we skip Foreign Cinema tonight and...eat in?"

"Hey, I was thinking exactly the same thing. I'm sort of hankering after some tube steak myself."

"I guess great minds do think alike," he said.

I smiled and looked into his eyes, so warm and trusting. That's when I decided I would tell him the truth about how I was inspired to shave *down there*. I'd apologize and promise to never do it again. The nosing around his computer, that is; the shaving would be on the menu for a long time to come. He might be a little mad at first, but he couldn't deny the benefits. Wasn't it worth a little snooping for me to get this enlightening little snatch of his inner life?

Besides, after what we'd just done in his office, I was sure he'd have to agree—sometimes good things can come from bad behavior.

TEACHING TERESA

Gwen Masters

I don't want you to do that!"

Trevor looked up at Teresa in surprise. He was poised between her thighs, his hands on her knees, naked as the day he was born, and obviously more than a little excited. His tongue had worked wonders from Teresa's neck down, and now that he had reached his obvious goal, she was freezing up.

"What's wrong?" he asked. He was truly puzzled. Teresa had been more than eager to drop to her knees and take him into her mouth. He hadn't even asked for it, but she had seemed to want it just as much as he did. Trevor was the kind of man who always returned the favor, and now that he wanted to, Teresa was stopping him? What wasn't making sense here?

"I don't like that," she blurted. She blushed a sweet shade of red, something that would have made Trevor smile if he hadn't been so stunned by her words.

"You don't *like* that?"

"No."

"But…" Trevor paused. He tried hard to think, which wasn't easy to do with most of the blood in his body rushing to places other than his brain. Teresa squirmed under him, but he didn't let go of her knees. Her expression was carefully guarded. Trevor tried to read it, but the truth was, he didn't know her all that well, not when it came to this. It was their first time.

"So you're saying you don't want me to go down on you because you don't like it?" Trevor asked slowly, as if he was making absolutely certain of the facts in this situation.

"Yes."

Trevor tilted his head at her and blinked a few times.

"Okay. You're going to have to explain that one."

"What is there to explain? I don't like it."

"But what don't you like about it?"

"I don't know."

"You don't *know*?"

"That's what I said!" Teresa was indignant now, and more than a little embarrassed. She blushed scarlet. Her ears looked like they were on fire. Her eyes were bright with either the edge of anger or unshed tears. He settled back on the bed and let go of her knees. She immediately pulled them together.

"I'm sorry," he said softly. "I just want to understand."

"There's nothing to understand. I just don't like it."

Her tone had softened, and Trevor knew he was finally getting somewhere. He studied the way she looked askance at him, the way she seemed to be hurt by the very idea of letting him go down on her, and thought maybe he understood after all.

"Someone did something that made you not like it?"

She shook her head.

"You've never done it before?"

She pulled the covers up over her. Trevor pulled them right back down. She shrieked in surprise and grabbed for a pillow.

He took it from her and promptly threw it off the bed. Before she could reach for anything else, he grabbed her hands and lay down right beside her, almost right on top of her. He carefully looked only at her face and nowhere else. Teresa buried her head against his shoulder.

"No wonder you're scared," he said softly.

"I'm thirty years old," Teresa lamented. "Most women have done this by now."

Trevor closed his eyes and sighed. "It's not a problem with *you*, Teresa. You've just met all the wrong men."

"But no man ever wanted to do it."

"*I* want to do it."

"Why?"

Trevor thought about that for a moment. What did he love about it? Why did he like doing it so much? Sometimes he even thought about it when he was alone, with no way to take care of the problem but to use his own hand and even then, the thoughts that made him come the hardest were those of a woman writhing in ecstasy under his tongue.

"I love everything about it," he told her. "I love the smell, that deep and secret scent. I love the taste. I love the way it changes when a woman comes, and the way it changes again after I've been inside her. It's like I can taste all the different levels of arousal."

Teresa was looking up at him with wide eyes.

"Most of all, I love the way a woman moves. I love the way the same touches can get a different reaction every time. But I also love finding that one thing that drives a woman crazy every time."

Teresa was looking at him like she hadn't ever seen him before. Trevor laughed.

"You really didn't think men enjoy that?"

"No," she said instantly, and Trevor knew she really believed that.

"Did you like going down on me?"

She smiled wickedly, some of her shyness gone. "Hell, yes."

"Then why is it so hard to believe I wouldn't like that kind of thing, too?"

Realization was suddenly dawning in her eyes.

Trevor crawled over on top of her. He kissed her softly, then harder, until she responded by bucking up into him. His lips trailed down, stopping with each nipple. He worked each one until Teresa was pulling his head harder against her. He abandoned her nipples to his fingers and started working his way down her belly. Her belly jerked with each breath. She shyly tried to close her legs, but Trevor moved between them and held them apart.

"Trust me," he implored. "Trust me, just once, and I promise you'll like it. I'll like it, too. I promise."

Teresa smiled down at him, even though she was blushing again. She lay back as his hands slid down her belly. Trevor blew his cool breath over her thighs until she quivered. Only then did he let his tongue touch the inside of her knee. His hands started at her toes and caressed all the way up. He took his time exploring every inch of skin from those toes to the bend of her thigh. By the time he was done, she was breathing hard and raising her hips into his touch.

Trevor slid his tongue along her lips. She shuddered and tried to close her legs. Trevor waited out the last-second indecision. Finally Teresa relaxed. Her legs fell open. She lay back and closed her eyes.

"Thank you," he whispered.

Teresa smiled. Trevor dropped his gaze to what she was letting him explore. He slowly licked around her lips, giving her plenty of time to stop him if she wanted to do so. From the way she was moaning, he was pretty sure she had been converted to his way of thinking.

When he dipped his tongue into her, she gasped aloud. Her motions went completely still. Trevor did it a second time, this time delving a little deeper, and she still didn't move. He looked up at her and saw a face full of bliss and discovery. She had never felt this before. The thrill of that made Trevor harder than he had ever been.

He played with her until her moans quieted down. Then he slipped his tongue up to her clit, and she immediately arched right up into him. There was no hesitation in the way she moved. She spread her legs wider and twined her fingers through his hair.

"Don't stop," was all she could manage to say.

Trevor closed his lips around her clit. She bucked so hard, he was almost afraid he had hurt her. There wasn't a single ounce of shyness left. He licked the tip of her clit with his tongue and swirled it around. He pressed down hard from time to time. He stroked her slowly, then quickly, and she wiggled around underneath him until he had to hold her hips to keep her from moving.

Every woman has a few little triggers, those things that work better than anything else, and Trevor had just found one of Teresa's. The pressure of his hands on her hips was what it took to send her into overdrive. She thrust up into him and he patiently moved with her. Nothing in the world could make him give up what he was doing. He kept up the pressure, kept licking and gently sucking, until Teresa suddenly stiffened underneath him. Her legs clamped hard around his shoulders. She squealed with delight as her clit throbbed under his tongue. Trevor let up a bit, knowing she would be sensitive, but he didn't stop moving his tongue until Teresa collapsed under him in a heap of exhausted pleasure.

Trevor pulled away with a kiss, and smiled against her thigh. He had been the first, and she had trusted him enough to drop all her inhibitions and come for him. The thrill of that was a rush of happiness that made him want her even more.

Her legs were open and she was more than willing when he moved up between her thighs. She reached down and touched his cock, and Trevor groaned. He was so hard it hurt. She guided him right to what he wanted. The first touch was almost more than he could take, and he told her so.

"Teresa, I won't last long. We need to slow down."

"No," she insisted as she smiled up at him. "You said you liked that. It was foreplay for you, too. I know you want to come, baby. And now it's your turn."

She thrust her hips up. He slid into her with one long stroke. Teresa kissed his throat and wrapped her legs around his hips. He wanted to slow down and let her come again, but he knew he didn't have the ability to hold back this time. He protested and tried to slow down, but Teresa again insisted.

"Come for me," she murmured into his ear. "You'll make me come again soon enough."

Trevor closed his eyes as she thrust up, grinding against him, driving him to the edge in a few short minutes. When he opened his eyes, she was looking up at him. Her eyes were bright with satisfaction. Her face was flushed. Her lips were open and swollen from his kisses. Her hair was tangled and her smile was mischievous.

"If you want to go down on me again," she said sweetly, "you'll come. Right now."

Trevor almost laughed out loud. At the same time, the orgasm overtook him. He shuddered in Teresa's arms as he came. She ran her fingertips down his back and breathed a satisfied sigh as he emptied himself into her with a long, low groan. When it was over, he collapsed on top of her, breathing hard.

"Wow," he said, and out of nowhere came the laughter. It took him by surprise. Teresa simply smiled at him and smoothed his hair away from his forehead.

"You really do like that, don't you?" she asked. He kissed her nose.

"Give me a minute and I'll do it again," he promised.

Teresa gave him that wicked smile he was starting to associate with very good, very naughty things. "You bet you will!"

QUEEN OF SHEBA

Jen Cross

You really wanna know about the best time? Well, there was this one guy, back when I was in school. But you have to promise you won't tell Max. Okay?

At first, I thought Jimmy was just really into foreplay. He'd say, "Can I touch you?" And before I was done nodding, he'd have reached out a calloused hand to my body, maybe resting it on one of my thighs or against my belly for a second, but he was always only interested in my pussy. His eyes would glaze a little, he'd moisten his lips, and get focused like a cat.

When Jimmy really got going, my pussy would feel like it was molten, you know? All melty and hot, like—well, I'm getting ahead of myself here.

Jimmy, with that mouth and tongue, those lips. He'd push up every single pillow behind me and set me back against them, prop my feet up and over to either side of my mussed single bed. After he'd sort of enthroned me, got my butt and hips propped up and thighs splayed, he'd just sit back for a minute and look at

me, those ruddy cheeks flushing and his eyes bright and almost—
if it weren't for that set of cockiness to his jaw, the way his grin
pulled a little too tight to one side of his mouth so you'd never
be sure he wasn't about to crack up—*almost* reverent.
He never did, though—never cracked up, never laughed at
me. He just liked to keep me perched on that edge of nerves. But
really, maybe I just couldn't read him, after all those months,
and there was something else altogether going on behind those
eyes and that half-cracked grin.

I can't even remember exactly when or how we met. We were
both scholarship students at a school full of kids whose parents
had been planning for their darling Jacks and Janes since the
moment of conception. I do remember him coming to meet a
study partner of mine who was in one of the huge survey classes
I was drowning in. I'll never know what it was he saw in me and
we never were much for talking, but a few nights later, Jimmy
showed up at my door with pizza and a couple of Dr. Peppers
and a small bundle of flowers that he'd picked on his way over,
snatching them from one of the university's landscaped gardens.
I was charmed—and a pretty horny and somewhat easy lay.
Thank goodness.

He'd look at me for so long that I'd start to cover myself sometimes—the staring was so unusual and here I was, a girl who
hadn't been much for nudity, even if no one else was around. In
high school, I'd been one of those girls dressing in the bathroom
stalls for the first two years, till my friend Jackson, you remember
him, pointed out one day that I had bigger tits than most of the
girls in my class, and that if anyone said anything it'd be out of
pure jealousy. I didn't exactly believe him, but I risked changing
by my locker finally and except for a wisecracked, "Well, shit,

look who's finally joining us out here," there were no other comments. I mean, what was I even expecting?

Except maybe how my mom used to cut her eyes at me when I'd be getting ready for school in the morning, wondering why I bothered with doing my hair or putting any color to my lips—looking like I thought I was the queen of Sheba, when I was really such a cow.

With Jimmy there was something else going on. He'd look at me like I was beautiful, the way someone pauses, kind of dumbstruck, before a stunning work of art or a breathtaking sunrise, stops to really be present with that spiderweb caught with morning dew stuck up there between the peeling paint and cracked window frame of your first apartment—you know. I mean, the only person who'd ever told me they thought I was beautiful was my dad, and that was when he wanted me to let him watch me in the shower. And then, in high school, if some guy liked you, you knew that as soon as he told you how pretty he thought you were, you'd hear him joking about you with his friends. I used to hate that feeling, how the big openness of longing and being longed for got dropped, reverted back into a kind of pit of loss and shame and embarrassment; when I realized that maybe they were just kidding after all—do you know what I mean?

But things with Jimmy were strange and different, and of course, he was hard to believe. When I tried to cover myself, he used to just say, "Wait—please, Steph," and even though I'd keep my hand on the sheets, I wouldn't pull them up over me, over my curves, the pushes of flesh around my belly, the little hairs darkening my thighs, or, sure, the split of my pussy or my breasts. Over the months we were involved, I got more comfortable, even sometimes spreading myself wider for him, more open—like I deserved to be so displayed, like I was exquisite, unique.

Sometimes he'd touch himself while he looked, his cock hardening behind the fabric of his boxers and khakis with its preternatural twitching, and I would clench inside myself, feel the rose blush spread from my chest.

Don't tell me you don't know what it was. I knew. But still, I loved it.

He'd brush his fingers through my thick pubic curls, loosening the free hairs, and then he'd bend forward, dive in. His body would sort of fold. He wanted inside me and sure I know that as a whole person, I didn't exactly exist anymore when he got into that wet fleshy focus, but at the same time I knew in that moment that I was being revered.

Now, like I said, I had reason in my life to believe that my body would never be reverenced, so when he put his mouth on me that way the very first time, when his throat opened and his warm, damp breath eased and heated across my pussy, propped up and open as I was in my little chilly dorm room, I just about started to cry. I mean, the wet prickled all around my eyes and my nose started to run. When I sniffled, Jimmy raised his eyes up to me sharply, not exactly in surprise, but not exactly knowing either. He just smiled, pulled one hand off my thigh and caressed my cheek.

"You are *so* beautiful, Stephanie—"

And this is what happened in my head: now, I know that I am supposed to be a self-actualized woman, and it doesn't matter, or shouldn't, whether a man wants me or not or thinks I'm cute, and yes, I know I'm smart and believe in the power of reasonable footwear and warm clothes in bad weather, and I was raised on feminism and will never disavow my own inner strength—but, and it kills me that this has turned out to be true—I got so wet when he said that to me, so thick and soft and open, so scared that maybe he didn't really mean it and, oh, I just wanted to quit thinking so much and feel what he was about to do.

Jimmy helped me with that right away, dropping his head back down between my thighs and letting his tongue smooth slow and wide up from the bottom of my pussy to my clit, and I gasped, let my legs fall farther open, which was nearly impossible. He'd ripple his tongue up across me, never exactly settling in any one spot but instead touching my whole pussy, all at once. Then he'd focus back in, suckling hard and fast, with such a quick change that I'd see stars and start to beat the bed.

My hips got good and stretched that season with Jimmy—he could spend a whole lot of time between my legs. At first, thinking he was just really into foreplay, like I said, I figured he'd give my pussy the same few licks and half suckle that my other boyfriends had offered, anxiously humping the mattress in anticipation of the real thing. But no. Jimmy languished there, lavished attention, bathed me in sensation and pleasure, built a kind of longing I hadn't known before—and, frankly, haven't known since. Now, that's just between us.

Jimmy would use his hands to hold me open, and his whole mouth, his nose and chin and cheeks. He'd fuck me with his tongue, then lap at me with the full flat of it, wriggle the tip across my clit, then capture the fat little head between his thin lips and suckle first gently, then more sharply, as I came. And came. And came.

He got me off so many times when he was down there, like that was the whole point. Can you imagine? He may have come in his hand or his pants sometimes—I never really knew; I was too busy screaming and lost in the pillows, grabbing his head, shoving my hips up into his face, sometimes capturing my tits in my own hands (if I wanted any other part of my body to get some attention, I had to give it myself; Jimmy was nothing if not focused).

I felt gluttonous, fat and lazy and joyful, those few months—
like I had something someone could gorge himself on, and yet *I*
came out the other side deeply satiated.

I offered to return the favor, though I was terrified he might
accept; I'd always gagged on boyfriends' cocks in the past,
and couldn't keep it up for very long in those days. But Jimmy
dismissed my offering, not as ridiculous, exactly—more like
something sweet but silly, like how your folks smile at you when
you tell them you're going to build them a big house on the
moon someday.

He just urged me to settle back and set himself to slowly
licking again, practically feeding, and I would close my eyes and
forget that any other kind of sex existed.

And even though things came to a near-screeching halt when,
first, Jimmy called me *Meredith* while his tongue was buried
thick between my pussy lips, and *then* when my coworker
Brenda started describing this great guy she was seeing, who ate
her pussy for hours and made her feel more beautiful than she
had ever imagined feeling, Jimmy changed something in me. He
opened me up to my body in ways I hadn't imagined before he
set me up on a throne of my own pillows, gently pushed my legs
apart and told me, before bending down at the waist so I could
watch his broad back and light curly hair descend onto me, "My
god, Stephanie—you are so pretty."

I get worked up about it even now—just look at my hands
shaking. He wanted to make all the girls feel beautiful, I guess.
After Brenda, I didn't return Jimmy's calls anymore, didn't open
the door for him when he came over. He left two messages on
my answering machine, though: the first one was so dirty that
I erased it before he was halfway through describing what he
wanted to make a date with me to do, and the second was so
simple: "Please let me see you, Stephanie. I miss how you taste."

It was so honest, I don't mind telling you, I got all wet just hearing those words. Maybe it was a mistake to pick my pride—or my self-respect, I'm not sure which it was—over the magic of his mouth. But what's done is done, of course. And Max and I have a fine time in bed. Nobody wants to be the Queen of Sheba all the time in bed anyway, does she?

SUSPENSION

Craig J. Sorensen

R emy rubbed his cheek again. His glossy smooth face still felt
foreign. He had even gone so far as to tuck his long curly
black ponytail under the collar of the blue blazer he'd scrounged
from the back of his closet.

Most potential clients seemed to like Remy's usual "artsy"
look. But Alexander Mollison was not most potential clients.
Thriving art careers had germinated under the attention of Alexander.

Remy followed the hostess to a table along the side of the
elegant restaurant where a portly, distinguished gentleman sat
looking out over the busy street. He looked every bit of his
seventy years, maybe more. His face was drawn and distant, his
chin angled from his skull like he was in mid-chew.

The man's eyes unclouded from their dreamy state. "Remy
Micheaux?"

"Yes."

"You're not what I expected."

Remy shrugged.

The gentleman waved toward the chair opposite him. "I'm Alexander Mollison, perhaps you have heard of me."

Remy took the seat. "Of course, Mr. Mollison. I'm honored you've—"

"I saw some of your pieces, and I found your attention to detail and traditional forms while keeping a dramatic, modern feel, appealing. This is what I require for this painting. I need something traditional, but updated. Detailed but with emotion. I wish you to capture the essence of a woman." Alexander's attention departed the building for the street again. His hard negotiator's gaze yielded to a tiny, longing smile.

"Any particular woman?" Remy broke the awkward silence.

Alexander's attention returned to the present. "You will do better to listen than to speak."

Remy's jaw clenched. He'd never dealt with a wealthy patron like Alexander. He restrained himself and nodded softly.

"I knew her back in 1958, and just briefly. She was very bohemian. Intelligent and eccentric. Erudite but simplistic. We lived in the same space and time, but we were going in very different directions. She was magnificent. Red hair, green eyes, fair skin, freckles. Curvaceous but strong. Youthful but wise." Alexander lifted one brow. "You have a question?"

"Do you have a picture of her?"

"No! I don't want a damned portrait. I want the feel of this woman, of this moment. I want the spirit. A magic moment. If you need some picture—"

Remy raised his hand. "No, I don't need a picture."

Alexander let the silence wash the space before continuing. "I spent only a few days with her, and we were—well—intimate just once. Just one magnificent time. It was in her crummy apartment. It was on an old battered black chaise in this tiny living room. She smelled of cheap soap and sweat. The loving went all too fast. Afterward, I sat on a wooden chair by the window. I knew somehow it was the only time we'd be together. When I looked back, I saw her lying like some sort of—well— artist's model."

A red 1956 Cadillac convertible passed and Alexander's eyes tracked it, seemingly transported. He returned to Remy. Hand gestures now accented his words like a deaf man making poetry. "She was beautiful. She sprawled naked, both sexy and innocent, and though we had just made love and I was—well—completely relieved, I wanted her all the more. But as bad as my mind and heart wanted her, my body would not...respond, if you know what I mean." He showed a rare blush. He focused on his half- empty martini.

Remy nodded sympathetically.

Alexander's face returned to its usual pallor. "I never saw her again. I will pay five thousand dollars if you can bring life to this memory for me."

Remy raised his eyebrows. It was the lot of the undiscov- ered artist to chase the dangled carrot. He still had to drive a cab to supplement the rent on his converted industrial loft. He had a stack of paintings in a dark corner of his studio to stand as witness that he had chased his fair share of carrots that got away.

But this was one big carrot.

There were those stories of Alexander seeing a commissioned work completed and doubling what he had originally offered the artist. But there were also stories of Alexander slinging insults and throwing a one-hundred-dollar bill. It was his equivalent of leaving a one-penny tip for a waitress.

Alexander stared as Remy absorbed the offer. "I'll make it ten thousand," Alexander concluded.

Remy looked in the man's steely eyes. It was a huge gamble, a ridiculous on-spec assignment. Remy felt his head nod. "Okay."

Alexander handed Remy a menu. "Order anything you like, my boy." There were no prices on it. If he got nothing else, at least Remy would get a good meal.

"You have finished my painting already?" Alexander's wrinkled face stretched with anticipation.

Remy crossed the long expanse from the teak double doors to the huge matching teak desk. "Not yet. I want to show you some roughs."

Alexander leaned back in his chair and his jaw tightened. His brow compressed as Remy opened a portfolio and produced six pastels. Each was a careful composite from photographs and paintings he'd assembled through meticulous research, and rendered with remarkable detail. Red-haired, green-eyed women, settings appropriate to place and time. Different poses, different lighting, carefully selected symbolism in the surroundings. Remy lined the drawings along the leather couch to the side of the desk.

Alexander's eyes deepened. "This is just like the other artists. These will never do!"

"They're only roughs. Are any of them close—?"

"There is no life in any of them. This is crap! You're just copying!"

Remy drew a deep breath, bit his lip painfully, and choked back the words *Fuck you, asshole,* in the depths of his throat. His words came out with a gentle quiver. "I'm only trying to get to your vision."

"You're the artist, not me. You have no track record, but the first three artists I went to were such disappointments. And these were formidable painters. Well, I'll be none too surprised if you can't—"

Remy held up his hand and gathered the roughs from the couch. "I can do it."

Disembodied words repeated gently in Remy's mind as he wandered. *Tell him to fuck himself. No, bow out gracefully, you're out of your league. No, tell him to fuck—*

He paused at an old diner. Inside an elderly couple at a booth studied dog-eared menus as they looked up at a waitress. Remy could see his reflection as his jaw fell open. The waitress had waves of bright red hair running down her back. Her body was curvy but a little athletic, with porcelain skin that supported a dusting of warm freckles. She glanced outside at Remy as she wrote down the old man's order. Her eyes were the color of polished jade. Her pink striped waitress's outfit was too big; she seemed so at ease, yet so out of place in it.

Remy went inside, sat at a booth, and waited. His leg bounced nervously.

"What do you want, hon?" Her name tag said MEGAN.

Remy looked deep into her eyes. If this beauty wouldn't satisfy Alexander, he was already dead.

Megan's eyes widened impatiently.

"Listen, Megan, this may sound like a line, but are you an actress or model or something?"

Megan snorted. "I'm a waitress, buddy. What d'ya want?"

"Roast beef special. But listen, what I wanted—"

"One roast beef coming up." Megan turned away sharply.

Remy choked the lousy roast beef down. He couldn't afford to thumb his nose at any meal. When Megan poured a second cup of coffee, he started, "Look, Megan, I'm an artist and I have this big commission—" Megan shook her head. Each time she passed him, he tried to introduce the subject without success. Finally, when she brought the check, he grabbed her hand. He handed her the last bit of money from his wallet. A twenty. "Keep the change."

"Look, this is too much. I'm not going to be a model for you, so let me just get you your change."

"Megan, I'll pay you well. Okay, not so well, but I will pay." Remy clung to her. She tugged her hand. Remy fell to one knee as if proposing marriage and let his arms flop like a rope bridge in the wind.

Megan laughed and let her arm fall limp with Remy's. "How much?"

"Fifteen an hour."

She pulled her hand free.

"Twenty-five an hour!"

She looked back at the counter, then back to Remy and whispered. "I won't do it naked."

Remy lowered his head. The roast beef wasn't sitting well. He raised his eyes again. "Well, it is a nude."

Megan bit her lip. "Fifty an hour." Her eyes locked stiffly on his.

"I can't afford it." He didn't want to admit he couldn't afford twenty-five. "But I'll be a perfect gentleman. No funny stuff. Twenty-five isn't chump change." He looked around the grubby diner.

Megan shook her head and walked away to ring up his bill. Remy slumped his shoulders and walked to the door. Megan rushed over and blocked him. She held out his change.

"Really, you keep it." He gripped the doorknob.

"What are the chances you'll pay me?"

He looked back and shrugged. "If I can sell the painting, you'll be paid very well. Every bit of the fifty per hour. If not I'll pay you what I can. I promise you that."

Megan looked him up and down. "You want me to do this on spec?"

Remy laughed. "Well, I guess you could put it that way."

Megan forced the change into his hand. "All right, when should I come?"

When Megan arrived at Remy's studio, he recounted Alexander's story. Her eyes traveled his studio several times as she absorbed it. "That's sweet. Kind of romantic."

"I suppose it is romantic in a lost hope sort of way."

Megan's mouth opened into a broad smile. "I know a little about that." She hesitated, drew a deep breath and unbuttoned her waitress's outfit deliberately. She slowly drew it off her shoulders, then modestly covered her underwear.

Remy wanted her nude, but he fought his natural impatience. "It's okay, we can start this way." Her shoulders relaxed in relief as he guided her with careful words. He found a good angle, as goldenrod evening light cast deep shadows around Megan's ivory flesh on the battered black chaise he'd found at a flea market.

For the first two sessions he worked with her in her underwear, perfecting the colors and shapes in pastel studies before blocking in the forms on the big, thirsty black canvas.

Megan began to undress, then paused at her underwear as usual.

"I think I need you to undress all the way this time." Remy framed the words gently.

Megan softly nodded. She drew a deep breath, then released her bra, exposing full breasts with small, bright pink nipples. Remy felt his cock begin to get heavy. She exhaled and pushed her panties down. A shock of bright red pubic hair stretched out. Remy turned around casually and pivoted his cock line parallel with his zipper. Not since his early days as a student had a model made him hard.

The pale, cool lines of Megan's body sprang to life on the canvas. Fading Dial soap, light whiffs of sweat, and greasy diner food mingled with oil paints as he began to focus on her details.

But as he created bright red curls of pubic hair, something felt wrong. He leaned back.

Megan twitched, ready to cover. "What's wrong?"

"I'm not sure, but please, don't cover up. You're beautiful."

Megan considered. "Well, they'd—they'd just had sex."

"Yeah," he replied blankly. The words turned over as his eyes settled on her bone-dry pubic hair. "What are you saying?"

"Well, I'm just saying—" Her face blushed sunrise red. Again she twitched.

Remy thought of what Alexander had said about the contentment of his bohemian woman. A conflict of his need and her satisfaction. He looked at the sprayer bottle he used for his plants. He approached Megan with a thought of adjusting her pose minutely. Maybe even spritzing her bright pubic hair.

He thought of Alexander's response to his composed samples and walked past the sprayer.

Artist and model remained as fixed as statues. Gingerly, Remy rested his fingertips on the middle of her silky thigh. Megan tilted her head sweetly and stroked the side of his hip. In perfect time, their hands moved toward each other's groins.

Remy stopped, but Megan splayed her fingers all around his crotch, curled them over his shaft, then under his balls.

A hint of Megan's vagina, earthy but delicate, colored the air. Remy's long fingers resumed moving up her thigh and combed into her soft pubic hair. Her eyes seemed conflicted, but her body opened wide. Her fingers clawed into the top of the chaise. She moaned as Remy rubbed her clit, then slid inside her growing wetness. Her face relaxed and her eyes closed. "Oh, yes. Make love to me, Remy."

Remy's free hand gripped his belt. But a tendril of reason invaded his consuming need. Tension. He massaged between her legs eagerly with both hands, spreading her warm juice. Her body became a coiled spring. "Please, don't stop!" Her hips crushed his fingers. Her jade irises glowed in the sunset light that cut through the sparkles of airborne particles released by her writhing on the chaise.

Her eyes locked on the bulge in his jeans. He fought his need to enter her—poured it into his hands and leaned his face within an inch of her pussy. Her hips tilted toward his face. The smell of her sex was appealing, but he'd never wanted to taste it on any woman. He kissed her pussy like a teenager on his first date and pressed his tongue to the back of his lips like a prisoner about to escape his cell, not knowing how he would navigate to the fence. Megan's fingers intertwined in his long dark hair.

His mouth slowly opened and she became breathless, silent. His tongue circled her pussy slowly, then traced the folds. She made a small sound and then her voice raised as he grazed her clit. Her fingers squeezed him tight to her pussy.

He didn't care for the taste, but he loved to see her body twist with pleasure. He channeled all his desire into satisfying Megan with his virgin mouth.

Megan's fingers joined in. Remy pressed his tongue inside Megan and he studied how her middle fingers stroked her clit. Her hips rocked gently as her orgasm washed down her body.

Megan lay, panting softly. Remy returned to the easel. With the grace of a seasoned artist's model, she fell into the position that they had composed the first time they'd gotten together. The moisture between her legs glistened, and her eyelids sat low.

Remy painted some details of her face and body in a wicked flurry. His hard cock became a comfort as he rendered her confidence and satisfaction channeled through his burgeoning need.

Remy was known for his meticulous research. When details were critical, research was key. Megan's response to his tongue drove him to the Internet. Search word, *cunnilingus*.

Megan showed no trepidation when she disrobed the next time. She sprawled on the chaise hopefully. He ate her more deftly, and led her to orgasm with little help from her fingers. The painting began to refine beautifully.

The time after that, she stripped her waitress outfit to reveal that she was nude under it. She patted the insides of her thighs playfully. When he knelt between her legs, something had changed. Her taste was now delicious. He pressed his lips tight to her, pushed his tongue deep inside, and her fists pounded the sides of the chaise.

He curled his tongue hard inside her and stroked her clit like her fingers had. Her eyes and mouth gaped. Her hand rested in the top of her pubic hair, then pulled back to the top of the chaise when he pressed his middle finger inside her. He patiently explored her vagina.

Until this moment, Remy had believed he was a good lover. He'd tackled numerous positions of the Kama Sutra. He'd learned to hold off an orgasm for long periods. But he had never known a woman's body like this. The objective had always been getting his cock to where it should be. No country roads and Sunday drives, just get on the superhighway and focus on the destination.

His second finger entered her and her mouth slowly stretched like a hungry gator's. His fingers curled forward in her as if calling her from across the room. Her eyes went wide when he found crinkly ridges at the front. She went still and deeply silent. He cupped her clit in his tongue then flicked it while his fingers pressed harder at the nub, varying speed and pressure. Her eyelids opened wide, cavernous pupils dilated. A shocked gasp escaped her parted lips while he settled into a slow, steady rhythm. He felt like a maestro conducting a symphony. He increased the pressure on her G-spot and flicked her clit. The deep sound of her ascending arousal accompanied the violent waves of her hips.

His cock throbbed, tingled, pulsed as he taunted her sensitive spots. Her body begged him to enter her. But he focused on each twitch until her face crushed tight and her fingers splayed wide, hands held out toward him as if imploring him to stop.

He didn't.

Her pussy squeezed his finger, her abdomen clenched like a bodybuilder's six-pack. A scream exploded from her nose and mouth. Fluid popped from inside her and splattered Remy's face.

Hot, divine nectar.

Remy sensed the might of her orgasm charging through his body—some sort of transference. He reached inside his briefs and felt the fresh warmth that had gushed from him unchecked.

"Oh, my god! What did I—?" Megan looked stunned as her legs collapsed down either side of the chaise. She looked at his soaked face apologetically as she gasped for air.

"Beautiful!" Remy rushed to the easel.

Megan started to move back into the pose they had composed on the first session.

"No, no, stay just like that!" Remy pulled down the carefully composed painting which was nearly complete and replaced it with a blank black canvas.

Despite his sudden orgasm, he needed her terribly. His tension was like the middle span of a long suspension bridge: perfect balance unifying divided shores.

Her bright red pubic hair sparkled. Remy's cock swam happily in the pool of semen that cooled on his hip. "Just relax, honey."

With a flourish of brushes and palate knives he created an expressive form of Megan's satisfied beauty. Impasto bright reds and greens were charged by golden highlights. The snowy terrain of her form with warm flecks was suspended on cavernous black. It swirled with passion and satisfaction and need suspended.

He was exhausted, as if he had finished a triathlon. Megan lay asleep, in the same sprawled position, with a contented smile.

Remy stared at the painting in surprise. It wasn't what Alexander had asked for. It was the most powerful painting Remy had ever done, and yet he knew it was inadequate to capture Megan's true beauty. He didn't care what Alexander thought. A hundred dollars, ten thousand or no pay at all, it was all the same.

Remy was already rich.

Megan smiled as she approached with a pot of coffee and a dog-eared menu. She held out the menu. "You want the roast beef special, hon?"

Remy waved off the menu. "I don't think so. Some tastes grow on you, some don't."

Megan's face turned red and she lowered her head. He cradled her chin. "Just coffee."

She poured the coffee while Remy pulled out a fat envelope. "And here's the tip."

Her eyes widened as she looked inside. "My god, that's—that's—" She started to count the stack of bills several times.

"Alexander was pleased. That's your half."

"It was never about the money, Remy." She tilted her head

to the side and held the envelope out toward Remy. He pushed it back.

"Fair is fair. The painting's done. Alexander loved it. Called it genius. He said it wasn't what he asked for, but was just what he needed, and he paid twice what he promised. It never would have happened without you."

She bit her lip.

"I don't need a model anymore."

"Okay. I understand." She nodded fatalistically.

"I won't have you be a memory I'm chasing fifty years from now."

Her eyes widened. "What?"

"Look in the envelope again, Megan."

She looked deeper in the envelope and found a freshly cut key, shiny as a new penny. She turned the key over in her hand, then slowly dripped it in her pocket. She set the fat envelope it in front of Remy. "Hold this for me, please. You sure you don't want something from the menu while you're here?"

"I'm saving my appetite."

KISS THE COOK

Giselle Renarde

H ow are eggs Benedict like oral sex?"

"I don't know, Lawrence. How *are* eggs Benedict like oral sex?"

"You don't get either at home," he chuckled.

You don't get either at home? My stomach plunged six stories. I guess he meant it as some kind of a veiled compliment, but still...Lawrence wasn't usually so crass. Even if the insult wasn't aimed at me, it still hurt to hear him say something so mean-spirited.

"Groan," I said, pretending to find his joke merely innocuous. "Somebody bring out the hook."

"The what?"

Looked like he didn't get my vaudeville reference. Why did I always do that? Pretend to be perpetually unoffended, I mean.

"Never mind," I conceded, kissing my way across Lawrence's fleshy abdomen. Nuzzling his pubic hair from top to balls, I took in that quintessentially male aroma of spent cock. Pure sex. Now that was good stuff. What a bad joke, though. So bad I couldn't relax after the rather incredible blow job I'd just given him. This time, I had to say something.

"I don't like it when you criticize your wife," I confessed, running my fingers through those curly graying hairs. Shaking his bald but beautiful head like he was scrambling eggs in there, Lawrence looked down at me. "It's very unbecoming," I continued.

"I don't know what you mean," he claimed. He *claimed.*

"Eggs Benedict? Look, I know you and..." I tried to say *Ruth*, but it just wasn't happening. His wife's name was the only taboo word in our repertoire. "I know you and she don't have a satisfying sex life...."

"It's not a matter of satisfying or unsatisfying," Lawrence interrupted. "There is no sex life. It doesn't exist."

Consumed by *schadenfreude* was the jealousy I'd felt a moment earlier. I was the only girl for Lawrence. Audrey LeBreton plus Lawrence Galloway equals ♥ 4-ever! At least that's what I chose to believe.

Laying my breasts on his exhausted cock, I hugged my man around his butt, rocking from side to side like a kid with a doll. "I'm so glad," I admitted. "I can't stand the thought of you..." I couldn't bring myself to say those words, *sleeping with your wife.* Eww! Gross! Yuck! It was like picturing your parents having sex. "Well, just imagine me having sex with another man."

"I can't," Lawrence replied, covering his ears like the *hear no evil* monkey. "No, the idea turns my stomach. It's...it's...upsetting."

That's when a thought occurred to me. "Hey Lore, if we follow your joke to its natural conclusion, it suggests nobody's getting any oral loving—not the guys, not the girls."

"Not the married guys and girls. Not at home, at any rate,"

he corrected my logic, but still didn't seem to understand what I was getting at: he couldn't complain about not getting it at home when his W word wasn't getting it either.

"I have trouble believing that's universally true," I disputed, kissing his pillowy belly. "But what the hell do I know? You're the one who's married."

Statements like these always resulted in silence. His silence was precautionary, anticipating an argument. Mine was sometimes contemplative, sometimes wallowing. That morning, I was merely reevaluating my position.

When the silence looming like rain clouds above our heads grew too cumbersome, Lawrence spoke up. "You know how you're always asking me if I have any fantasies?"

"...And you're always telling me all your fantasies are memories of our lovemaking? Yes, I know. You're so boring that way."

"I'm sorry," Lawrence began with that trademark kicked-puppy expression on his face. "But I think you'll find me less boring after today. I finally thought of a fantasy."

He'd been fantasizing about me? Oh, my insides shivered with anticipation! What would it be? A bit of kink? Role-play? Something involving a whip, perhaps? Or whipped cream, at the very least.

"I'd like to shave your pussy."

What?

"You want me to shave?" I whimpered, combing my darkish pubic hair with my fingers. It was neatly manicured. Well, not perfect, but it was certainly no briar patch. "Why? What's wrong with me? You think I'm too hairy?"

"No, no, of course not," Lawrence consoled me, running his hands through the mess of hair on my head. "See? This is why I didn't want to tell you! I didn't want you to take it the wrong way."

Shaking off the initial hesitance, I had to remind myself that a good mistress is up for anything. And I'd always been a good mistress....

"Okay," I began, falling right back into the realm of uncertainty. "But why, if you don't think I'm too hairy, do you want me to shave?"

Lawrence smiled affectionately, his eyes all tenderness and light. "No, Audrey, it's not that I want *you* to shave. In my fantasy, *I'm* shaving *you*."

Oh. That put an entirely different spin on the matter. He wanted to shave me! How kinky was that? Perhaps Lawrence's mind was every bit as filthy as mine, and he just did a better job of hiding it.

Hopping out of bed, I squealed, "Let's do it!"

Plus on est de fous, plus on rit!

In my little white bathroom, I fished a new razor from the cupboard while Lawrence set one of my thick burgundy towels over the lid of the toilet.

"Have a seat," he bid. "Do you have a set of manicure scissors?"

Plunking myself down on the towel, I grabbed the tiny shears from a dish beside the sink. Lawrence sat his naked ass before me on the ceramic tile. Under the bright fluorescent light, he stared straight into my cunt as it unfolded like a moist calla lily.

"Some women might be embarrassed sitting like this," it occurred to me.

"Are you?"

"No." Petting the soft hair at the back of my man's head, I truly wasn't. "You think my pussy is attractive, right? So I don't mind."

"I think your pussy is beautiful," Lawrence agreed, kissing

my pubic hair softly. My insides tingled with anticipation until I was tempted to drop my body into Lawrence's lap and fuck his brains out right there on the bathroom floor. But no. *La patience paye.* Waiting for my dessert would only grow my desire.

Lawrence started out tickling my front by clipping the darkish hairs. When he was finished, he grasped me by the ankle and placed that foot on the side of the bathtub. His noble face was so rapt in concentration, the lines deepened around his squinting eyes and suddenly he appeared much older. It gave me an idea of how he must look at work, nose stuck in a book, taking in all that information. *Ostie*, was he ever smart! Even as he brushed the dark hairs from my abdomen, Lawrence looked like a genius.

To protect my tender flesh from the sharp manicure scissors, Lawrence set a full finger firmly down on my wet pussy lips. My body fluttered like it was being carried to Mexico by monarch butterflies. I couldn't help but tremble.

"You have to keep still," Lawrence scolded like those students at the haircutting school where *Maman* took me as a child. "The last thing I want is for you to get hurt."

"I know, but it's so hard," I whined. "Every time you touch me, I just want to grab your cock and ride it 'til you come!"

Lawrence smiled that smile he smiles when he's trying not to smile. My bashful *chum*! Not so bashful right now, though, snipping with great care at the hairs along my slit. I could feel my pussy muscles grasping, praying for action, with every crunch of the scissors. Maybe he could slip one of those handsome fingers between my wet folds, just to tide me over?

But then my bald beauty placed the scissors back in the bowl. Rising to his feet with an amount of effort befitting a man of his years, Lawrence ran some water into the basin and dipped in the razor, swishing it about. I don't know what I must have looked like, but he asked if I was nervous.

"I don't think so," I replied, staring at the three razor-sharp stainless steel blades. "I know you'll be careful."

Grabbing the shaving gel from my shower, he replied, "I shall treat your body as if it were my own."

"I know you will. That's why I love you."

Dampening my facecloth in the sink, Lawrence laid it over my pelvis like he was tucking a doll into bed. The warm water soothed my flesh like a tender massage. Lawrence circled the cloth around a bit, pressing against my mound. He kissed me fleetingly before removing the sopping fabric. Ah, *que c'était bon*!

As Lawrence sprayed some berry-scented shaving gel into his palm, rubbing it into the very short hair of my pubis, I nearly jumped again. That gel felt cold against my warm flesh. *Merde*— I would have to contain myself if I didn't want to get nicked by those shiny metal blades! With nothing to take hold of as the razor approached my naked flesh, I bunched up the burgundy towel in my hands. *Please don't cut me,* I tried to telegraph to him, even though I knew he wouldn't.

Squeezing my eyes shut as the razor met my skin, I could only tell where Lawrence had shaved by the cold lines it left down my front. I heard him splash the razor in the basin, then retrace his steps with more warm water and shaving gel. When I opened my eyes, my mound was pristine but for the hair surrounding my slit. Lawrence admired me tenderly, smoothing the warm cloth against my skin, tracing his finger along my jawline, then along the curve of my breast. His work was breathtaking.

"You're not finished yet," I said as Lawrence set the razor down.

"I'm not?"

"You're not," I declared, opening wide my legs. "You have to shave between my thighs as well."

"*Mais oui!* But of course," Lawrence imitated my accent. Like he would have forgotten! Now that we were halfway through the task, I was getting really into it.

I got that same butterfly feeling, even more intensely this time, when Lawrence pressed his fingers over my pussy lips to guard them. Oh, if that man didn't fuck me soon...

"How did you end up with a fantasy like this?" I asked, trying not to shudder as my delicious *chum* dragged the cold razor through the dip between my thigh and my mound.

He was silent for a moment, deep in concentration, trying not to injure me as he shaved. Massaging shaving gel into the other dip, he dragged the razor up that side too. I held tight to my towel. When he got up to rinse some water through the blades, he finally answered my question with "I don't know."

"You don't know? How can you not know?"

"I don't know."

An enigma, that man. As shadowy as I perceived myself to be, I was nothing of a mystery compared to my Lawrence. Clean razor in hand, he shaved every last hair from around my slit with swift passes of the blades. I'd never been so nervous and so turned on at once. With my pussy pumping out clear nectar, those full fingers pressing my lower lips could easily slide and...

"Close your eyes," Lawrence bid, and I did. The hot washcloth pressed upon my mound once again, and my temperature rose to greet it. It was unbelievable how fresh my skin felt, unhindered by all that hair. I felt virginal, somehow, like pubic hair represented my sins, and now all were gone.

"Open them," Lawrence cried, voice brimming with glee. He had my handheld mirror between my legs so I could get a good look at his handiwork.

"*Ah, come c'est beau!*" I applauded, leaning forward to kiss my happy puppy. Never in my life had I felt so bare, so utterly and completely nude. It was a freeing feeling.

"You're pretty as a picture, Audrey. Pretty as Venus riding that clamshell."

My bald beauty always knew exactly what to say, but sometimes I got stuck. Sometimes I wasn't so fluid at changing gears from *Français* to English. That's when I wound up saying things like, "You're pretty too, Lawrence."

As a final treat, my darling man would wash my soapy self down in the shower. Let me tell you, when he cupped my ass with one hand and set the warm water from the showerhead against my pussy, I thought I would come on the spot. Maybe I did, I don't know. After running that water over my thighs and my ass until all the gel and bits of hair were gone, he teased my tits.

Hooking the showerhead back into the bracket, Lawrence took a seat on the tub ledge and just looked at me facing him against the white tile wall. "How did you become so beautiful?"

Ah, my heart fluttered. "Years of practice."

Lawrence chuckled, gazing at my nubile cunt. His adorable expression modulated, becoming rough and eager, until my man was growling like a black bear. He reached toward me, two fingers extended the way the British flip the bird, and pressed my shaven pussy lips tightly together. My glistening pink clit popped out from between the two snow white slopes as he pulled my juicy sex to his mouth. Nearly tumbling over, I had to catch the soap dish to keep steady. Lawrence slid his strong fingers up and down on either side of my shaved lips, the pressure causing me to cry out. *Tabernacle*, was that hot!

Slumped over my cunt like a scavenger greedily consuming some morsel of flesh, Lawrence had never appeared so much the red-blooded male. When he lolled out his tongue and pressed it flat against my white mound, still pressing either side, I was near ecstasy. His tongue was so close, so beautifully close to my skin without all that hair in the way. That hot slab of mouth meat traced its way up my smooth lips, showing no regard for my bulging clit. Oh, my knees just about gave out when he did it again. Lawrence had never given me head this forceful, this animalistic. His untamed tongue was making me wild. As the warm shower beat down against my straining breasts, I wished he had a head full of hair for me to latch on to.

Finally, Lawrence showed some specialized attention to the tip of my clit, sticking out from between my pussy lips. He licked it, repeatedly, his tongue flat and firm. With my free hand, I pinched my nipples so hard I shrieked with delight. That's when he released my cunt from his mighty grasp and my folds spread in every direction like a tiger lily. Grabbing my thighs, he licked again, long and hard, right against my juicy hole. *Ostie! Tabernacle!* What an animal Lawrence had become!

Like a lion devouring a gazelle, Lawrence slurped up my nectar along with the shower water streaming down my stomach. Sipping my juices, his chin glistened when he looked up at me, fire blazing in his sky blue eyes. Oh, there was nothing hotter than a fierce gentleman whose mouth gleamed with pussy water—nothing hotter in the whole, wide world.

And then came the sucking, the sucking, the slurping sucking, and it was so unfathomably good I thought I would die. The arch of my pussy lips, culminating in my clit, seemed to be absorbed somehow, or stuck beneath his soft pink upper lip. *Ostie et Tabernacle*, the suction was like nothing I'd ever felt, like a black hole was consuming my body clit-first.

"*N'arrête jamais de me lécher!*" I cried.

He didn't stop licking me, but I doubt if that was because he understood my French. Lawrence growled and the vibrations sent shivers through my core, reminding me how empty I felt.

"Keep growling, and finger me too," I instructed like this was life or death.

Sucking hard on my clit, growling at my naked flesh like he might tear me to shreds any second now, Lawrence launched a manual assault upon my swollen cunt. One, two, three fingers thrust in my pussy, and then four with the pinky. Who ever said men can't multitask? While Lawrence drew my clit between his teeth, clamping down like a wild thing, I pinched a nipple between my fingernails and that was the very most pleasure my little body could tolerate. My cunt went into spasm, locking down on those four fingers, sending waves of pleasure skipping across my abdomen until I cried out with joy. *Tabernacle!* Nothing on earth could possibly feel better than this, I was certain.

Turning off the shower, Lawrence toweled off my spent *corps* and carried it back to bed. I didn't say anything for a very long time. I was too tired to speak. My brain was fried. Fried eggs. This is your brain on cunnilingus. Maybe I had a little nap, but sometimes it's hard to tell whether you've been sleeping or just resting your eyes.

"You were making little noises," Lawrence told me when I regained consciousness.

"Snoring, you mean?"

"No," he said. "They were like little sighs of contentment."

I nearly blushed.

"You were an animal today. I've never seen you like that before."

Lawrence shrugged. "I was inspired, I suppose. I got to fulfill my one and only fantasy."

"Was it as good as you imagined?" I asked, no longer curious as to why he desired to shave my pussy. That was a marvelous adventure!

"Better!" Lawrence assured me. "Hey, I have a little extra time this morning. How about some breakfast? I'm starving after all that..."

"Wild-hot animal sex? Yes, me too. But we'd better go out if you're craving eggs Benedict. I'll give you anything you want in bed, *mon amour*, but don't expect me to cook for you as well."

HAPPY HOURS

Adelaide Clark

It's only after two months of fucking around the clock that I discover how truly submissive and slavish Pete is, not to mention a complete slut for eating pussy, the kind who salivates at the mere mention of the word, his taste buds *and* his cock going into overdrive as he imagines nestling his tongue against a woman's wetness. Sure, on our first date, he got down on his knees and kissed my four-inch patent leather boots, then licked his way from the tip of one to its upper edge. He sucked the heel once he'd taken the shoe off for me, moaning in pleasure while I held it above him, dangling it like a treat before a dog. He especially loved it when I scraped its sharp point across his tongue, his lips pursing in ecstasy. He was like a male Linda Lovelace, a guy with a pleasure switch in his throat, just waiting for someone to shove something in there to unlock it.

My pussy lubricated itself in anticipation of that divine tongue entering me, but first I made him treat the other shoe to its own tongue-licking. Then he had to pay homage to my breasts, and boy, did he do a good job. Pete did everything he could think of to my nipples: licked them, flicked them, nipped them. He buried his face between my breasts while I slapped his face, then forced him to take both nipples at once. I was the one making him bite my nipples so hard I wanted to scream, but make no mistake: I was never his sub, and never would be. Other men have gotten me to be their pretty helpless princess, tied up and tortured, flogged and fucked, but with Pete, we always know our roles. They come so naturally I sometimes forget that I've ever been anything but a top.

I made Pete wash his mouth out—no, not with soap; that would be a little too cruel, even for me—but with wine, a bottle of white I'd been saving for a special occasion. I'd just gotten my pussy waxed, relishing the sharp, tingling pain of the gentle-voiced Russian woman pouring the hot blue wax onto my sensitive skin, then ripping the stubborn hairs off my most tender parts. I always long for someone to lick me clean when I'm done getting waxed, for a warm, willing, pliant tongue to treat me to its curling, cunning caresses.

I had to wait a few hours for our appointed date, but Pete gave me exactly what I was looking for. He made love to my newly sleek lips, found countless ways to get to know my insides, to press gently against that one spot that drove me mad before making a merciless drill out of his tongue and plunging it in and out. He sucked on my clit like he'd sucked on my nipples—hard—just the way I wanted him to, without even being told, the barest hint of his teeth connecting with my nub at the exact moment I needed something more intense. My pussy spoke to him in its own magical voice, the pairing of my privates and his pursed lips a match made in sexual heaven, while all I had to do was watch, if I chose, or shut my eyes, sink back against my expensive leather couch, and feel his wet heat invade mine. He did such a good job that I'm not even sure how many times I came, only that by the end, my heels were digging into his lower back, my just-long-enough fingernails scraping his head where the short tufts of hair did little to protect him, as I thrust upward into his face until that wasn't enough. When that moment came, I sat up, kicking him to the ground, and sat on his face. I slid along his tongue, suffocating him for a few seconds before letting him up for air. Watching him gasp in arousal and surrender was as enjoyable as the feel of his stubbly chin when I moved downward onto it. Pete was a pro at pussy-eating, the kind of man who seems born to have his face buried between a woman's legs, which gave me an idea. I was going to a convention for dominant women—some professionals, some like me who simply came to the lifestyle after discovering none better. These were women who wore their superiority like a fine mink coat, something a little outrageous, a little unacceptable in polite society, but nevertheless coveted by men and women alike. They turned heads no matter what they were wearing, their innately triumphant strides signaling to the lesser minions that they were in control, always, while scening or not. These were women who could snap their fingers and command those around them, strangers and acquaintances, to come running as fast as if they'd cracked a single-tail whip. They were powerful and, trust me, they knew it. We knew it, I should say, since I count myself among this special coven's most prized members.

Though they were my peers, my friends, my confidantes, we were all competitors on some level. We may have preached all sorts of things about live and let live, *laissez-faire* sexuality, and consent, painting a portrait of one big happy, kinky, twisted family, and we were, in a way. But in another way, we were all sisters vying for the most attention, the best slaves, the biggest harem. We wanted to impress each other with our outfits, and with the men who carried them for us. Walking into a ball-room with one man shackled, collared, and crawling next to us was fabulous, but walking in with two or more trailing us on leashes was something to stop drinking champagne and coo over. I'd gotten just as caught up in keeping up with the mistresses as anyone, even though I didn't do it full-time, and sometimes I needed a break from all the rules that world seemed bound to. But for the purposes of the upcoming convention, I knew Pete would be perfect. The perfect pussy-eater, one I planned to provide for a very special show—and tell. Or rather show and feel.

I broached the subject as I lifted myself off his mouth after what had to be at least orgasm number four. My cunt was raw, almost bruised in that way it can get after a good fuck, a happy kind of soreness, the kind you miss when its twinges disappear. "You like having your mouth full, don't you, Pete?" I asked, casting my eyes about for something else to shove between his gaping lips.

"Yes, Julia; I mean, Mistress, I do," he said, stumbling over his words in his eagerness.

"Hmm..." I replied absentmindedly, pressing two fingers into his mouth and watching as he swallowed them whole. His pants were straining with the pressure his hard cock was putting on them, and I was almost surprised he hadn't come yet. "I have a little proposition for you. I want you to be my sex slave for the weekend, two weeks from today. We'll be heading to Houston, and I'll pay for your flight from New York. You'll be mine to do with as I please, and what I want to do with you is have a daily happy hour, after the workshops. For those who want something they can't ask a bartender to pour them, at least in public." I added another finger, and his eyes widened. With my other hand, I ran a nail along his neck, making him squirm. I shifted, pulling my fingers out with a smacking sound from his lips, so I could press my palm against his erection, letting him know I knew it was there, and that I knew I was causing it.

I slapped his dick lightly before continuing, pinching one nipple while I spoke. "You'd pretty much be eating pussy for an hour or so, maybe two if there's enough demand, and you wouldn't necessarily know whose lips you were servicing. I'd keep you naked, blindfolded, and hungry, and women could come in at any time during the appointed hour and you'd have to lick them until they were satisfied. They could touch you if they wanted to, under my supervision. You'd also be fair game to me, so if I wanted to spank you or tickle you or fuck your sweet little ass while you were busy eating, I could. And if the mistress of the moment wants you to throw in a few extras, like rimming or some finger-fucking, you'd have to comply. Basically, your mouth would be mine—and any other woman's who wanted it."

I unzipped his pants and freed his cock. He didn't speak, even though nothing was stopping him. I wrapped my hand around Pete's cock and lightly stroked him, filling him with more imagery as ideas occurred to me. "Maybe two women will both require your attention at once. You'll lie on your back on the bed, and while one plays with herself, the other gets on top of you like I just did and fucks your mouth, dropping down onto you, then sitting up, close enough for you to smell her, to feel the warmth of her wetness, but not close enough to taste. Then the other decides she's gotta have you and gets on top, pressing her thighs against the sides of your face. Maybe you'll know it's a different woman, maybe you won't. But no matter what, you'll have to tongue them like you just did me. If they give you specific instructions, you're to abide by them—or else."

Maybe he had just reached that penultimate moment where

there was no going back, or maybe the threat of some abstract punishment gave my horny little slut what he needed, because at that, he came all over my hand, his cock pumping out wave after wave of hot cream. "Open wide," I said as I made him lick it all off my fingers, then scooped up the rest as best I could and fed it to him. "I bet you like boy come, too, and maybe if you do a good job, another time I'll let you play with some of my gay friends. But for now, I think my colleagues will really appreciate using your tongue to unwind from a long day." I smiled, already printing up the elegant invitations in my mind—thick black card stock with raised silver script:

You're invited to
A Very Happy Hour
Presented by Mistress Julia
Prepare to be pleasured as slave Pete attends to you orally,
for as long as you need.
First come, first serviced.
Every day of the Convention, 5 p.m. – 6 p.m.
Room 621
No RSVP required

"Well?" I asked, pinching the skin along his shaft lightly, but hard enough to get Pete's attention. "Are you in or out?"

I knew that a man as orally skilled as Pete, who was clearly the apotheosis of submission, would never turn down the opportunity to both be my knight in shining pussy juice, as well as partake of the opportunity to serve multiple mistresses. I was right. "Yes, Mistress Julia, of course, anything you say." I hadn't started out as "Mistress Julia," but when he'd simply blurted it out one night while I was on top of him, fucking him so hard we almost broke my bed, I realized I liked its ring. Usually, I don't go for the formal nomenclature, the sadistic semantics of kink. It's enough that I know which guys like to be beaten and which don't. But Pete was special, and I was going to prove it. "Very good," I said, standing and nodding at him to get up. "We have work to do if we're going to get ready. I'll email you tomorrow about the party invitations, and give you a checklist of what you'll need to bring with you." This wasn't strictly necessary, as really all he needed was that sweet, sweet tongue, but I wanted to delegate the invitation task to him, and put him through as many paces as I could.

As soon as he left, I phoned my best friend and partner in kinky crime, Meredith, and we gossiped about who would be first in line to partake of Pete's services. Some dommes are simply greedy, not content to exploit their own posse of pussy pleasers, but wanting to exert their power over others' subs as well. I liked the idea of having someone with me who other women lusted after. It wasn't so much about cattiness or showing off, as it was pride. I'd taken men to these conventions before, but they were my private boy toys. I may have paraded them around, but our play was something intimate between just the two of us. We'd go to parties but more as voyeurs, filing away what we saw before us to possibly use later.

This time, I'd be instigating what could be a convention-wide pastime, something that would be talked about on message boards long after we departed. As selfish as that may make me sound, I also knew that for a man like Pete, this was a fantasy come true: seemingly endless pussy to eat, a Sisyphean sexual task that would never truly be over. I wanted the taste of pussy to remain on his lips, to linger in his mouth, to stick to his tongue from his morning coffee to his last bite of dessert. I wanted him to wear pussy perfume, to bask and bathe in it, to wear out his lips until they were chapped and tired. I wanted him to show these women that any boasts about his gustatory prowess were all true. I'd found a man who not only loved to go down on women, but seemed like he just couldn't get enough. I wanted to find out if that was, indeed, true.

I emailed him with my instructions, typing out the party invitation from memory, but adding another hour onto the time. He'd get a break, of course, but one hour would be merely a tease, especially with two hundred women slated to show up that weekend. If that many were joining us, chances were an hour just wouldn't do justice to Pete's tongue, and we couldn't have that, now could we?

I called and booked a room with a single king-sized bed, figuring that if I wanted him to, Pete could sleep on the floor. He likes that every once in a while, and I always let him back up between my legs in the morning. I made sure the room was ample enough to accommodate several people and various positions, because some ladies find pussy-licking an activity best saved for furniture other than a bed. This one had a desk with a sturdy office chair as well as a plush chair a lady of leisure could sink into, spread her legs, and wait for a man like Pete to get on his knees where he belonged and open wide.

I had been tempted to create a registration system, because I'm nothing if not a control freak, and I knew that if twenty women were dying for the chance to get eaten out by my slave, I'd be wet with anticipation. But the uncertainty of the situation, for both of us, turned me on. I didn't have to try to keep anything secret from Pete; his free-for-all mouth was public knowledge. And when we got there, we found that word had indeed spread. Upon arrival, I was greeted at the desk first by the unctuous host, then by a woman of my acquaintance, Patricia, a thin, almost bony but surprisingly strong domme who greeted me with a brittle hug and then squeezed Pete's face so his jaw opened, running a finger along his lower lip. "Very nice," she said, turning to me to deliver the compliment.

"Thank you," I replied, reaching for Pete's ass, which was clad in a pair of threadbare jeans I'd selected especially for their holes, which allowed me to easily reach inside and cup one of his cheeks while still making some perfunctory nod to modern fashion. "I take it we'll be seeing you later tonight," I said, raising my eyebrows as I felt more eyes turning toward us.

"Indeed," she said, and when she walked away, I settled my hand more snugly against Pete's ass. I happened to know from previous observation that Patricia was quite the squirter, the kind of woman who could ejaculate practically on command. For some men, that might be a punishment, but with Pete, it would be nothing but a reward, the kind I didn't mind offering to him. After all, he was in my service all weekend, and he should at least be able to partake of some of the "happiness" of our happy hours.

Soon, it was time for the moment I'd been particularly looking forward to, the rest of the convention seeming to fade into obscurity. I prepared Pete by having him drink from the bowl of water down on the carpet. He's not a puppy, but I wanted to make sure he got into his role. Oh, and he was naked, blindfolded, and wearing a studded collar. I wanted to watch him use his mouth, his tongue. I almost ordered him to practice on me, but since I had no idea how many women would come through the door, I refrained.

Soon, promptly at five, the doorbell rang. I was only sad that the carpeted floor prevented my five-inch heels from clicking, the hypnotic sound that is almost Pavlovian to many slaves, Pete among them. I knelt down before him, then slapped him across the face, lightly enough not to leave a mark, but hard enough to get his attention. "Are you ready to give that tongue a workout?"

"Yes, ma'am," he said seriously. Another bonus to keeping him naked was that I could see the erection bobbing beneath him. I kissed him, unable to resist those lips, thin yet promising. I sank into the kiss, not overtaking his mouth like I normally do, but allowing a kiss like a normal boy and girl, not domme and slave. Sometimes, especially as a prelude to a kinky scene, a little vanilla is needed to spice things up. I opened the door, with Pete at my heels, to find Nadia, who looked every inch her Russian heritage, proud, tall, and fierce. She was over six feet with gleaming, glossy black hair, and when she opened her fur coat, she revealed that she wore nothing underneath. I was almost sorry to keep Pete blindfolded, but I also knew that even the sight of the most beautiful supermodel couldn't compare to the images he could work up on his own, and the uncertainty and humiliation his position put him in. And that's what I like, what really gets me off—watching him do things he would never do on his own, all because I say so.

"I'm ready," she said, then laughed, an imperious, booming laugh. She walked right up to Pete and introduced herself, holding up her foot and offering him the heel to swallow. He did, immediately, fellating the spike and moaning as he did. Just when he was getting into it, she pulled it out.

"Make yourself comfortable. What's mine is yours," I told her, and then it was my turn to laugh. He didn't know who Nadia was, so for my purposes, she was still a stranger to him, even if he did know her name.

I made myself comfortable, sliding a minivibrator out of my purse and putting it to good use while Nadia did the same to Pete. She was seated on the bed opposite me, while he was on his knees. To me, out of all the positions for pussy-eating, that's the best one, because it really puts the licker in his or her place. It lets them know that their job is to be on their knees, in service;

if the hands go behind the back, like Nadia had ordered Pete to do, it only further reinforced their roles. Of course then he lost the use of his hands for additional stimulation, but from the way she grabbed his head and shoved him into place, I didn't think that would be a problem.

"Eat me until I come," she said, and I leaned back and watched, lazily letting my body move closer to climax. I wasn't in a hurry, and watching him was like having a front-row seat to the perfect kinky film. Seeing Pete actually eating out another woman brought a rush of excitement to me. I watch him go down on me all the time, but this was different. He was doing it under my orders, and doing quite a good job from what I could see. Some of the view was obscured by the fact that he was trapped between her legs. She alternated between spreading them wide and pinning them tight against his ears. I was slamming my vibrator against my clit, the delicious sound of Nadia's juices connecting with Pete's tongue filling the room, when the doorbell rang.

I turned off my toy and got up to greet Virginia, a shorter woman with giant breasts that were bulging out of a corset, with nothing underneath. She'd put on a trench coat to walk down the hall, but had opened it when I opened the door. Ringlets of red hair cascaded down her shoulders, and a quick glance down below showed that she had those same fiery hairs there. "You better hurry up," I warned Pete, even though really we had as much time as necessary.

"Welcome," I told Virginia. "Make yourself at home." To tell the truth, seeing her spilling out of her corset and the way she smiled at me, I got a little hungry for her myself, but I didn't want to disrupt the flow of our evening.

I went over to Pete and placed a hand on his ass, squeezing hard. He moaned into Nadia's pussy, and she and I shared a look before I let my fingers drift to his asshole. I played with him while he slowed down enough to figure out just how to lick her to get her to come, with some guidance from her along the way. When he found that special spot, the room became quieter as he focused entirely on her. She had tossed her head back and when he finally achieved his goal, she flopped in her chair, arms wiggling, as a grin spread across her face.

Pete emerged sticky with her juices. I pulled him to me for a kiss, vicariously tasting Nadia before giving her a peck on the lips. "Someone else is here to see you now," I said to Pete.

"Lie down on the bed and get ready to be smothered," she told him, and I noticed his semihard dick pop straight into the air. He loves when he has no choice but to breathe, taste, and smell only pussy, when a woman uses his face for a fuck toy. I watched her mount him, but then had to tend to a stream of visitors, until four more women had joined us. I served them drinks as some chatted, while others observed Virginia riding him like a cowboy. The moments when she'd rise up to give him a chance to breathe also allowed us a glimpse of his pussy-smeared, blissful face. He looked like he was getting treated to manna from heaven, and in a way, he was. She rubbed herself against his chin and nose, then fucked herself for a second with two fingers shoved inside, before removing them and planting herself back down.

She rocked against him, and he endeavored to keep up. The ache between my legs was strong. The smell of pussy in the room was intoxicating, as was knowing that my very own slave was servicing some of the most sadistic women I'd ever met. "We want to go together," Amber said to me, indicating a domme she sometimes did sessions with, Lillian, while Virginia's wild red mane bounced along with her movements.

"Two at once, I like it," I said, grateful because the clock was ticking and Pete still had four more women to tongue-fuck. Plus, I could see that Amber had several silver rings dangling from her labia and a piece of jewelry hanging from the hood of her clit. I wondered what Pete would make of that; he was used to me au naturel.

"Yes, you horny brat, shove that tongue inside me," Virginia said, pausing a moment to pinch his cheeks. She then rose and turned around so she could straddle him from the other direction, pinching his nipples and giving him the scent of her ass right up his nose. This position also afforded us a better view, and I smiled as I saw her pink cunt lips connect so intimately with his mouth. Soon she was grinding back and forth in a way that probably chafed—not that I'd ever feel sorry for Pete. There's a glorious joy in being used for sex when you want to be, and Pete knew it. Soon Virginia was coming onto my slave's face, sinking down softly to let him gorge on her musk when she was done.

She got off the bed and sank into the chair I'd occupied earlier, while I again kissed Pete and praised him for a job well done. "You've got four more women to cater to, and then me," I said, surprised to see that only thirty minutes had gone by. Time flies when you're at a pussy-eating orgy, I guess. He turned his head in my direction adoringly, then grinned and licked his lips. "Amber and Lillian are ready for you now," I said, and they got up on the bed and spread their legs simultaneously. This was a catch-22 because he couldn't literally have his mouth on them both at once, and whichever one he neglected would surely want to punish him for his transgression.

Pete began with Amber, licking tentatively along her slit, clearly not sure what to do with the rings. "Tug on the rings with your teeth," she rasped, and he did, while next to them, Lillian held open her pussy and circled her clit with one finger. I could tell she was already plenty wet. "Now suck on my clit.

Wrap your lips around it. Treat it like a cock. Don't be gentle,"
said Amber.

I enjoyed watching him struggle a bit to relearn what was
inarguably his greatest skill. I couldn't see every detail that I
longed to, because of their positioning and my need to enter-
tain Patricia, who'd arrived looking like the cat who was about
to swallow its favorite canary, and a woman I had never met,
named Isabella. When she said hello, her voice was quieter, with
a hint of a Spanish accent. Most dominant women were loud,
with booming voices, so her seeming shyness was alluring. We
alternated chatting and watching, until finally I felt I had to step
in. Pete was switching off between Amber and Lillian, but not
getting too far with either. I poured some lube onto my fingers
and began teasing his back door.

"Maybe you need some encouragement, my dear," I said.
He turned toward me, but, being blindfolded, couldn't see me,
making the gesture all the more futile. "Keep going, I know you
know what to do." As I started to enter him with one finger,
he moaned, and his face entered Lillian more deeply. I felt like
I was fucking her by proxy. He sucked her steadily until I had
two fingers solidly up his ass, before he moved on to Amber.
Lillian played with her clit when she wasn't kissing Amber. The
other women in the room had stopped talking, transfixed, until
Patricia asked, "What will you do with him if he can't make
them come?"

I pretended to think about it, midstroke, but I honestly didn't
know. Lock him up in a cage? Deny him my pussy? Banish him
from my presence? None of those solutions were ideal. "We'll
cross that bridge when we come to it—or rather, when we don't
come to it," I said. That must have sparked something in Pete,
some primitive instinct, because the nature of his pussy-eating
changed. I don't know exactly what he was doing differently,

but I could feel it and sense it from the women's movements. They seemed to sink into the bed and each other, and Pete began fingering one while eating the other, moving his tongue and fingers in tandem. When Amber came, the room burst into applause, and she helped Pete out by teasing her friend's clit until she too humped upward, then grabbed Pete's head to her sex.

When they were done, the women got up, and I let Pete rest momentarily before giving him to Patricia, the squirter. I doubted he'd have recognized her voice, and I hadn't told him about her proclivity for gushing. He'd find out soon enough. "Put him wherever you want him," I told her, so she did—on his knees, face upward, while she straddled him. She had to hold on to the headboard for support and he had to kneel just so, but they could do it. She stood, with my slave directly beneath her. I liked the ingenuity she was displaying, and I sat on the bed close enough to observe. Patricia proved true to her word, and after only a few minutes, she was practically crushing his head with her thighs as she showered him with her juices.

Then it was Isabella's turn. I'd found out that she was new to being on top—she had worked as a professional submissive before now. Perhaps that's why her requests—for his blindfold to be removed, and for them to do sixty-nine—were so unique. Since she was the last woman to be serviced that day—it was well past six by then—and I had said that the women would be in charge, I allowed it, even looked forward to it. She was apparently an equal-opportunity oral sex fiend, because I recognized her lust for cock immediately. She made sure Pete was doing his part, but she swallowed his dick like an oyster, opening her mouth wide to take the entirety of his sex inside. They were perfectly in sync, as if they'd been mouth-fucking for years. I was almost a little jealous as they stayed coiled together for another half an hour, leaving only me as their audience. Isabella flopped back against the bed when they were done, letting us admire her plush curves, the tangles of curls between her legs; her rump in the air as she lay on her stomach, arms folded beneath her. "Well? What'd you think?" I asked him.

"I think...I'm hungry," is all he said before placing me back in the reclining chair and going so slowly I wondered if he was tired. But no, it was all part of his charm, wooing me with his tongue, making me very, very happy.

The rest of our happy hours were filled in much the same way, and for the final one, Pete was very busy, and we had several extra hours to kill so I extended the session, not wanting to turn away any pussy in need of some licking. Sure, some of the women got greedy, going twice, and some I knew were freshly fucked, but a woman can never have too many orgasms, right? I got so worked up during each one that I also put him to good use myself, not wanting to miss out. In between, attending workshops or parties, I noticed that we were truly the talk of the convention, with whispers and fingers pointed toward us, the women extolling the extraordinary talent and stamina of my slave. He deserved a medal, but not the traditional kind. I was going to reward him with a gold ball—through his tongue. Because, as the saying goes, too much of a good thing is wonderful, and when that thing is your slave's hot mouth on your pussy—or someone else's—it goes double.

SPILL

Alison Tyler

Spill it."

Morgan can tell when I'm upset. He reads my body language effortlessly. Sometimes, he knows I'm upset before I do.

"Come on, Lacey. Tell me what's bothering you."

He wraps his arms around me, presses his lips to my neck, lets me feel the safety of his strong, hard body. His voice goes lower than ever, and he repeats those two little words: Spill it.

"I don't know," I say, lying as he turns me to face him, feeling unsure of myself. What's on my mind? What whirring thoughts are keeping me from relaxing, from kicking my feet up on the coffee table and letting the day's stresses slip away? Too many to name, to categorize, to share.

"Let me help," he says, and I watch as he pours me a glass of white wine, hands me the stem of the glass, and then leads me to the sofa. He sits me down, his dark gray eyes never leaving me, even as he lifts his own drink to his lips. He's waiting for me to spill. I can tell. But the worries and tangles and stress that I feel

are all coiled in knots inside of me. I take a sip. I try to think.
I'm at a loss.

I am the sort of person who uses bonds—invisible but oh, so
real—in order to keep my feet anchored on the ground. What
are my invisible bonds? Routines. I know how my days look
weeks in advance. I can rely upon working out with my trainer
each morning at six. Having lunch with my best friend every
Tuesday at one. Drinking cocktails with Morgan each evening
at seven.

If I know what to expect, I can handle anything.

Surprises are what knock me off my axis, sending me spinning. And surprises are what I had to deal with today at work.
One unexpected issue after another. But Morgan kids me about
my need for routines. He will make fun of me if I share these
trivial details, if I do what he's asking. If I spill.

Morgan strokes my hair, bends down to kiss me. Peace flows
through my shoulders, relaxing them. Kissing him warms me
all over, as ever, but I know that's all we'll be doing tonight. We
never fuck during the week, only on the weekends. This is one
more thing I can count on, one more of the invisible bonds that
keep me in place. Our sex life is so hard-core, so deviant, he
knows I can't handle the power of it during the week, can't piece
my fragile self back together to carry on my workweek. We save
the heat for the weekends.

Then suddenly he is on me. Lifting me to my feet, carrying me
down the hallway to the bedroom. I'm too surprised to fight—to
even think of fighting. My mind is consumed by the fact that in
his haste to pick me up, he made me tip over my glass, and my
wine is now spilling in steady drips onto our carpet.

I hardly feel the motion as Morgan tosses me down on the
mattress. It's as if I can hear the drips of wine meeting the cream-
colored carpet in the living room. How grateful I am that I was

drinking white—always white—less of a chance to stain.

Seltzer. That's the word that comes to mind—how I may dab up the spill with a bit of fizzy water on a soft cloth. This is what I am thinking about while Morgan binds my wrists to the headboard. Clearly, he's been doing some preplanning as well. Will the stain come out if I pour club soda directly onto the carpet? I wonder, not challenging Morgan as he blindfolds me, then draws my yoga-style pants down my legs.

Then a new thought bubbles free: should I tell him that it's not Friday?

No, he must know what day it is.

Should I ask him what's going on?

No to that, too. Because he's the one in charge, and this is the thought that helps me to bite my tongue. I don't have to worry—Morgan has a plan.

He undoes the buttons on my cardigan with slow precision, his breath warming my skin as he parts the halves, then pushes up my tank top, revealing me. The room is warm, and yet a chill works through me as he starts kissing his way down my body, from my lips to that delicate inner curve of my neck, to my collarbone; down to my breasts, alternating from one to the other, and along my belly until my hips begin moving on their own. Gently rising up and falling back on the sumptuous comforter cover, begging in their own way for Morgan to give me what I want.

There are no words at first. Morgan simply plays me, using his fingers, and the palms of his hands. He is gentle, sweetly touching me to bring me pleasure. The bindings are the only part of the action reminiscent of the type of sex Morgan likes the best. I use invisible bonds to get me through the week—but Morgan uses real ones during the weekend.

And now I wonder: Is he really going to climb between my

legs and let me lose myself in the pleasure of his mouth? Without any twinge of pain first? Without any sort of warning? I can feel my chest tightening, as I wait for the real Morgan to come out of hiding. We've never simply fucked. He's never only bestowed pleasure upon me. There is always pain first.

But slowly, when he doesn't move, I start to relax.

That, of course, is the moment he strikes. He leaves the room, leaves me bound and blinded, and I wonder—desperately, jaggedly, if he has gone to wipe up the spill. And then he is back, and I hear the sound of glass being set on the table near the bed. My ears perk. My body tenses. Next, I hear him unscrew the cap on a bottle, then liquid pouring, and the sound of him taking a sip. He's gone for his scotch. He is going to watch me tremble while he enjoys his cocktail. Is that the game?

No. That's not it. Because finally, and with infinite care, he sets the base of his drink down on my flat stomach. And then he gives me the opposite command from the one he had in the living room. No longer does he want me to spill my worries for him, to spill the secrets that make my muscles tense. No longer is he trying to fix me with words and kind caresses. Now, he says simply, and softly: "Don't let it spill," using his strong fingers to spread apart my nether lips. Bringing his mouth so close to me. "I've just refilled my glass. I don't want to lose a drop."

Ah, fuck. There is no way.

Moving a little faster now, Morgan begins to lick at my clit. Usually, when he dines upon me, I have clips attached to my nipples, or clamps on my pussy lips. I have been spanked or paddled or thrashed with his belt. I have taken the pain and earned the reward. But now—this is a new game, a new test. All the worries of work have disappeared. All the things that bothered me on the ride home today, have vanished.

There is only me—with a glass balanced on my flat stomach—

and Morgan, who is clearly doing his best to make me spill.

He licks my pussy lips apart. He draws his tongue down the center of my body. He uses all of the sweetly naughty tricks that I like the best, moving faster and then slower, alternating in speed and in pressure. But in a way, I can't feel anything. Yes, I know what he is doing—almost as if I am watching from outside my body. See the pretty lady on the bed. Her shirt pushed up, her sweater dangling from her shoulders, her wrists cuffed to the headboard. Oh, she is fine, and lithe, and young, with dark hair and a dark heart. But what's that trembling on her belly? A beautiful cut crystal glass filled nearly to the brim with imported scotch.

If I'd told him about my petty grievances when he asked, would I be here now? If I'd bitched about my boss, or been catty about my coworkers, would he have petted my head and clinked glasses with me, and let the day end as usual?

I don't know. I don't know anything anymore.

All my concentration has been captured by keeping the glass still. This means I am tightening the muscles of my stomach, focused entirely on how that glass feels resting there. I'm suddenly grateful for the hours I spend in the gym, for the way I can control my muscles now after doing countless sit-ups and crunches until I am sore. The way I can make my belly behave is something beautiful to behold. The glass feels larger than I know it is. I am lost in the coolness of it, the weight of the liquid within. I wish I could watch, but the blindfold keeps me in the dark.

Morgan continues to work me with finesse, using two fingers to stroke on either side of my clit, his tongue tapping in the most desirable rhythm. Oh, fuck, he knows how to please me. His tongue laps hard and then soft, fast and then slow. He makes circles and diamonds, shoots ducks in a row. He does loop-the-loops and figure eights and on any other day, I would have come by now. Instead, I am giddy with desperation, and sweat beads my forehead and the nape of my neck. I wish I could wipe my brow with my forearm, but I am bound too firmly, and I daren't move a muscle.

His tongue trips over my clit, and I cry out. "Oh, fucking god, Morgan, please."

"Please what?" he asks in his calm manner, as if my pleasure is his ultimate concern. But it's not. We both know that. He has told me not to spill his drink, and he is going to make me do just that. No matter what I do. No matter what I say.

I am in a different zone, completely consumed by my mission. But why?

He hasn't told me what will happen if the glass tips. He's simply said not to let the liquid spill. My thoughts begin to pick up again. Like a crazy person, manic, desperate, I try to convince myself that I might like what he has planned for my ultimate failure even more than what he might have in store for my success. What if he's simply going to give me a spanking? What if he's going to wash my mouth out with soap? Take me into the bathroom for an enema? Try out his new bamboo cane? My mind spirals with images, visions of what could possibly happen next.

Then Morgan suddenly overlaps two fingers and thrusts them inside of me. I gasp, shuddering at the sensation, that feeling of being filled so delicious that for one beat I forget the glass— remembering just in time to tighten my muscles once more. Hearing the liquid slosh slightly.

Hoping that not a drop has escaped.

I feel Morgan's eyes on me, and I wonder what he's thinking. He laughs, low and soft, before returning to the sweet way he'd been touching me before, licking and kissing. Oh, his lips on me;

full, hungry lips, taunting me with the gentle quality of his tongue before taking a break and lifting the glass from my belly.

I sigh loudly, relief flooding through me. I am incredibly wet, both from the magic of his mouth, and from the excitement of the game. Morgan has to know how totally aroused I am. Shivers run through me. I'm shaking the way I do after a really intense workout. I sigh once more, and wait for Morgan to fuck me, pinch me, slap me, anything except what he actually does.

He sets the glass back into place, almost casually resting the base on the flat expanse of my belly once more.

"I'm going to make you come," Morgan says. "You know that, don't you?"

I nod, my whole body tense again. I listen as he refills the glass while it rests on my belly. I hear the cap, feel the weight change as the liquid rains down.

"It's expensive scotch," Morgan continues. "I'd hate to waste it."

I force myself to be obedient once more. His tone alone warns me. He does not need to use any threats of punishment. Unfortunately, he's letting my mind spell out what he might do if I let him down. And that's far worse for me than if Morgan had simply explained from the start the pain he would mete out for failure. What if he keeps me chained to the bed all night? What if he refuses to fuck me for a week? What if? What if?

And yet I can hear the humor in his voice. He's in a playful mood. This is a game, a drinking game, Morgan style. That fact isn't lost on me. It doesn't make me any less serious about not letting him down, but I appreciate the sound of the smile in his tone.

Once more, Morgan begins to lick me. And once more, all of my muscles go into lockdown as I do my best not to fail. But as his tongue makes those sweet circles around my clit, I catch a glimpse of my future: my hips rising, the glass tipping, the amber liquid pouring down my pale skin, and Morgan—not wanting to waste the precious liquor—drinking up every drop of my spill.

RAIN CHECK

Emerald

I felt Luke's hand between my legs almost immediately as I slid into the passenger seat. I gasped and bit my lip, turning to him with a surprised smile. He didn't look at me, just sat with a contented look on his face as he guided his SUV out of the parking lot. Our lunch date at the state park near our workplaces hadn't been quite as successful as we both would have liked, a fellow park patron walking his dog having happened by just as I was bent over a picnic table begging Luke to fuck me. As we'd walked back to the vehicle, I'd slipped the condom I'd transferred to my jacket pocket back into my purse, reluctantly accepting that we'd have to take a rain check.

Luke, however, wanted to make the most of the little time we had left together before we had to go back to our respective offices. I had worn no panties for our little tryst, so it was easy for him to delicately caress my clit now as he watched the traffic in front of him. It wasn't near rush hour yet, but there were plenty of other cars reflecting the afternoon sun around us as we stopped for a red light.

I put my sunglasses on. I was starting to squirm in the seat now, in part to keep my wetness from getting on the leather underneath me. I turned to look at Luke again. He glanced my way and smiled casually, appearing not at all out of the ordinary, I was sure, to the numerous drivers and passengers surrounding us who might glance out their windows and have no idea that his fingers were working me into near oblivion beside him. I wasn't quite close to coming, but his slow massaging felt so good I almost felt like I was floating. I would have been perfectly satisfied if he had said we were taking a road trip to Alaska, as long as he was planning to keep that hand where it was for the duration.

The light changed, and he accelerated with everyone else. I pressed my head back against the headrest, letting out a tiny moan as I gave up trying to keep the seat clean and relaxed into the leather, knowing a mess was already being made though I hadn't even come.

Finally he spoke. "I've been told, Renee my dear," he began, glancing over his shoulder as he merged into the left turn lane, "that I'm even more effective with my tongue than my fingers. So if you're enjoying this…" He trailed off as he removed his hand momentarily to make the turn, his eyes on the road ahead.

I caught my breath at the suggestion. Luke repositioned his hand and accelerated to cruising speed. I swallowed and looked away shyly. I didn't consider it in my nature to be shy, especially sexually, but on that subject it was undeniable that there had always been a mysterious hesitation in me. We had been dating for four months, and this was the first time the subject had come up so directly. I'd had the impression a number of times that he had wanted to go down on me, but I had always managed to divert his attention and avoid the subject.

It occurred to me that perhaps the time had come for me to suck it up and deal with it directly. Squirming a little for reasons other than the pleasure between my legs, I said uncomfortably, "Well..." I didn't get much further for a few moments.

He looked my way, eyebrows raised over the lenses of his sunglasses, waiting for me to continue.

I fidgeted with my fingers. "I don't usually let people do that," I finally finished.

He nodded slowly, eyes on the road, and said, "Any particular reason?"

I fidgeted more. There wasn't really "any particular reason," except for a vague self-consciousness that I didn't really know the origin of, much less how to explain in this context. In conversation, I had no trouble spouting off about gender and how women weren't socialized to embrace their sexuality, and specifically how oral sex on women being much less talked about and more socially taboo than oral sex on men was an example of that, et cetera—all of which I believed, but it didn't seem to fit the context when I found myself in the midst of this uncomfortable conversation. Furthermore, I didn't like to think of myself as being in the category of women who had any trouble embracing their sexuality. It was hard not to conclude, however, that the self-consciousness I felt about the topic at hand was an indication that socialization had gotten the better of me somewhere along the line. It was an idea I entertained with no pride whatsoever.

I returned to the conversation. "Um...I just...I don't know." The more I wasn't coming up with anything comprehensive, the more self-conscious I was getting. As well as frustrated—we'd been together for four months, for crying out loud. Why would I still feel uncomfortable about this?

"I guess I don't understand why you'd want to," I blurted

out. I felt like a traitor to my sex as I said it, but having no sexual attraction to women myself, I had never understood how the act could be appealing.

He chuckled. "Don't you like to do it to me?" he asked.

"Yes," I answered immediately. And I did. I loved to give blow jobs, craved it, salivated for the feel of his cock in my mouth and hot come shooting all over my face.

"Then what wouldn't you understand?" Luke altered the motion of his finger on my clit just enough to make me catch my breath before I could answer.

"I just...I'd have to feel like you really wanted to do it," I said finally. "I wouldn't want you to do it just because you think I want you to. I'd want you to really *want* to do it." I took a deep breath. I wasn't sure that even made sense to me, much less to anyone else listening. We'd stopped at a red light again, and Luke took the opportunity to look at me, lowering his head to meet my gaze over his sunglasses.

"Okay, well, I'll tell you this right now. I won't keep harping on it in the future, but I want this to be clear to you: I always want to." The words sent a jolt through me, and I almost came right then. He continued without breaking his gaze. "That's not ever a question. It's something I love to do, and I've been thinking about doing it to you since the first time I saw you. It's up to you—but don't ever let my desire be in question."

The cars in front of us started to move, and after holding my gaze for another beat, Luke turned back to the road. I shivered a little at the intensity of his gaze as well as at his words, and suddenly I found myself turned on by the idea like I had never been before. We were quiet for the five remaining minutes of the drive back to his office, his finger gently stroking my clit until he pulled his hand away to shift into PARK.

When I kissed him good-bye, he said, "I was thinking. Since

our park escapade was so abruptly interrupted today, I'd like to take you back this evening when we might be able to…finish what we started." He winked at me, and I grinned back. "We'll just try to find a spot a little less populated this time. I'll be wrapping up about six—can you meet me back here after you get off work?"

"Sure." I got out and wiggled my hips to adjust my skirt, feeling the slickness between my legs as I turned and walked to my car. Looking back once over my shoulder to catch Luke watching my ass, I laughed and blew him a kiss before dropping into the driver's seat.

Returning to the same parking lot a few hours later, I again felt the wetness between my legs, just from thinking about our earlier encounter. I watched Luke emerge from the building and then met him at his vehicle. He kissed me and threw his briefcase into his backseat, and I once again positioned myself in the passenger seat, smiling a little as I thought of our ride back earlier in the afternoon. We inched through rush hour traffic until he turned off the main highway to the road that led to the state park.

He parked in a different lot, smaller and farther back in the woods, and we got out under the shade of a cluster of huge oak trees, the sun almost completely blocked by the branches above. I grabbed a blanket from the back and followed him along a trail beneath densely packed trees. Eventually there was a clearing where the sun blazed uninterrupted to the ground a bit off the path. A huge rock sat on the far side of the grassy hill, and we crossed over to it and spread the blanket at its base.

Making no pretense of eating this time, we fell to the ground, kissing hard. Luke rolled on top of me, pinning me down as his lips moved to my throat, working their way up my neck until they found my ear.

"I want to lick your pussy," he whispered, and I jumped ever so slightly; partly, I couldn't deny, because of the eroticism of the comment. My pussy, without any input from me, got wetter at the words. In the next instant, however, I felt the familiar self-consciousness sweep in and overwhelm me.

Luke pulled my chin firmly with one finger to make me look at him when I ducked my head. "You don't have to let me if you don't want to. If you don't want it, that's fine. But please don't say no because you think *I* don't want to." He traced his finger lightly from my chin down to between my breasts, raising goose bumps all over my body. "Because I'm begging you," he continued softly, flicking his tongue out to touch my slightly open lips. He moved his mouth to my ear and whispered into it, "I want to lick you to climax."

My breath caught. "I don't think you'd be able to do that," I managed to get out. "No one ever has…" Internally, I knew that might be because I had allowed very few people to try—and when I had, I had been so uncomfortable that I had known from the start that there was almost no way I was going to come.

"Then just let me lick it," he breathed into my ear, his hand snaking between my legs to my naked pussy again. I was wet from the conversation, and my breathing deepened as Luke started circling my clit again with his finger. "I want to taste you." Gently he pushed me back on the blanket and started to move.

"No," I said suddenly, sitting partially up. He looked at me.

"Why?" he asked evenly, his finger returning to my clit. "Is it because of what you want or because you're worried about what I'm thinking?"

We both knew the answer, and Luke didn't wait for me to give it before moving to position himself between my legs. I was still propped up on my elbows, looking anxiously at him as he stared at my pussy for several seconds. I bit my lip.

Finally he looked up at me and smiled softly. "Your pussy is so gorgeous," he said. I looked at him, wondering if I could dare to believe him—dare to allow myself to relax and trust that he loved this, that he wanted to do it. That there was nothing to be afraid of. In that split second as I looked in his eyes, sure that he knew what I was thinking, I felt myself lowering back to the ground, my legs opening almost imperceptibly farther, nonverbally giving him permission. Giving myself permission.

Luke moaned against me as he replaced his finger with his tongue. I stiffened for just a second, some vague nervousness resurfacing in me, but he put his hands gently on the insides of my thighs, and I felt the reassurance in them. Relaxing again, I closed my eyes and let myself experience, let myself feel what was happening just like I did when he fingered me or fucked me or all the other things I loved when he did them to me.

Without even realizing it I stopped worrying—his enthusiasm was so evident. My attention then went to the sensation in my clit, the way it felt as his warm tongue feathered across it, my hands in his hair and both of his on my thighs. I arched my back as the floaty sensation returned and flowed through me, a comfort I'd never felt before when receiving oral sex.

As I started writhing, Luke pulled back an inch or two and whispered, his hot breath against my pussy, "I want you to come." As with our earlier conversation, arousal shot through me at the words, but at the same time my nervousness returned.

"Huh-uh," I whimpered, trying to raise myself up again.

"Mm-hmm," the sound vibrated against my pussy as he sucked my clit lightly. The sensation made me weak, but I couldn't stand the thought of coming while he was down there. I had been known to squirt, and the thought of making a mess all over him mortified me.

"No, Luke, stop," I pleaded, my voice weak but the intention sincere. Luke pulled away enough to look up at me.

"Renee. Please. I don't want to stop. Seriously. I want to make you come," his tone was pleading as well, but I couldn't handle the idea yet. I shook my head.

"No, honey. I'm sorry."

After looking at me for another few seconds, Luke sighed and hoisted himself back up to lie beside me.

I felt myself blushing. Luke ran a finger along my cheek and said, "Thank you."

"For what?"

"Letting me do that," he answered.

I looked dubious. He raised his eyebrows.

"Did you really like it?" I asked almost inaudibly.

He let out a short laugh. "Was it not obvious that I loved it?" When I didn't answer, he said my name, and I looked at him.

"I loved it," he said, looking into my eyes.

I took a deep breath. It was hard, actually, not to believe him.

"Now let me make you come," he said suddenly in my ear, moving back down between my legs before I even realized what was happening.

"Luke—no! Luke," I gasped as he pushed his face into my pussy again. "Luke—honey, stop it!" I heard the urgency in my voice. There was a serious possibility that I would actually come soon, I knew. I didn't think it would happen without an active psychological release on my part, but I still didn't want to take the chance. I tried to pull away but Luke anchored his arms around my thighs and held me in place as he ran his tongue frenetically over my clit. As I felt myself on the brink and tried to resist, he looked up and said, "Come for me, Renee. Now. I want your come all over my face."

And I was too far gone for the worry to supersede the erotic jolt of his words this time. He returned to my clit, and in another spilt-second decision I let the wave come, feeling the orgasm burst throughout my body as I screamed and bucked, his tongue pulsing in place and his arms tight around my thighs. I didn't squirt, to my relief, but I was immediately overcome by confusion, self-consciousness, ecstasy, and something I didn't even recognize as the orgasm ended, and as Luke once again rose to lie beside me, I found myself in tears.

He was quiet as he watched them fall. He wrapped his arms around me, and I cried as freely as I had come, letting what was there come out as it needed to. Soon I was still.

Luke asked me if I was okay, and I smiled because I knew I was. I didn't know how to explain to him yet that the mix of intensity, intimacy, and pleasure had simply overwhelmed me. And somewhere in there too was relief, though I didn't know how to explain that yet either—even to myself. I touched his face lightly and then pushed my head into his shoulder, pressing against him as he squeezed me and stroked my back. I felt him kiss the top of my head, then pull away slightly.

"Oh—we've got company," he said, sitting up and pulling my skirt down quickly. I turned and saw a young couple with an energetic lab on a leash walking the path a hundred yards away. "What is with the dog-walkers today?" he continued as I laughed. "I guess that's what we get for continuing to do this in parks. Think they saw us?" he asked, turning back to me.

I looked into his hazel eyes, the answer in me long before I voiced it.

"I hope so."

TREATMENT FOR A TONGUE JOB

Thomas S. Roche

s that fucking thing on?" she asks petulantly, from the depths of utter blackness.

"I think the battery's dead," he says, befuddled, which is why when the black goes away and she comes into view on the computer screen, she's got a look half of pity and half of self-satisfaction, and the black disk marked PANASONIC lies perched like a happy-face between her thumb and index finger.

"If you're going to invade my privacy," she says, leaning into the camera so her attractive countenance fish-eyes *Blair Witch* style, "Kindly remove the lens cap." She turns and pads naked toward the bathroom, her fine ass swaying just a little more than usual.

"Oh, I'm not invading your privacy," he says, following her into the head. "Am I?"

She bends over and turns on the water; the camera takes a long slow stroke up the back of her leg, the auto-focus going in-out-in, blurry-clear-blurry-clear on her pussy. Without looking back she reaches over her shoulder and flicks water at him. Her middle finger glistens upright in front of the droplet-flecked camera. "Just ruining my senate career," she says. "Fuck off." "Oh, come on, you love it," he says as she climbs into the shower. "It's like one of those POV pornos." The camera points toward the floor; he grabs toilet paper and daubs the lens off. It leaves a weird smear as he points the camera back at her. She stands there, water cascading over her naked body and steam wafting all around it; though she's flipping him off again, this time with both hands, she hasn't pulled the shower curtain closed and in fact seems provocatively poised, with one hip cocked and her body angled attractively.

"You wish," she says, her voice like melted chocolate. "Twenty minutes of head and a facial cumshot. As if. Fuck off."

"Yes," he says. "I do wish."

She flips him off again but still doesn't pull the curtain closed. In fact, as she drops the bird and makes an "eat me" gesture, groping her crotch, that middle finger performs an interesting function, wriggling between the lips of her sex and sliding inside while the auto-focus goes all wacky on the splashing droplets all around it. She does that for quite a few long luscious moments as the other hand takes the soap and begins to lather her belly and then slowly travels up over the swells of her breasts, lingering on her hard pink nipples before continuing to her neck. He zooms in on her foamy breasts; when he lifts the camera to her face, she has a sex-mad expression, almost certainly feigned, which, when coupled with the flat, soaked mat of ash-blonde hair, makes her look midway between a half-drowned kitten and a mermaid with love on her mind. This tempts him inches closer, just close enough that she can lean forward and plant a big wet kiss right on the lens, cackling wickedly as the camera goes waving all over the place, and he desperately starts to wipe it off with wads of toilet paper.

"Hey!" he bleats. "This is expensive electronic equipment!" He trains the camera back on her naked body. Her ass drips soapsuds as she bends over to lather her calves, something he's never seen her do before—it seems like a calculated move to tempt him closer, which this time he doesn't fall for. Thank god for 10x zoom.

She stands, stretches under the hot water, looks over her shoulder at him with a slightly depraved look. "You know," she sighs, "if you're so hot on making a porno, you should let someone ruin *your* future senate career."

"Huh?" he asks.

She bends over nice and slow, letting his zoom lens get a good view of the lines of her upper thighs, ass, pussy and lower back. She has to raise her voice to be heard over the sound of the cascading water.

"How come all those pornos have the guy holding the camera? That means he always gets all the head," she says. "I think we should make porn where *you're* the one on camera. It'd be a big hit. Pervert girls like me would love to see a cute guy putting his mouth to good use for a change."

She straightens up and turns toward him just as the camera goes down, clutched at mid-belly and pointing uncontrolled and forgotten at the floor.

"Really?"

There's a long pregnant pause, broken only by the whining hiss of the auto-focus going in-out-in as it alternately blurs the glistening tip of his soft cock and the Chinese character tattooed on his thigh: longevity, or "soft chicken" if you believe the urban legends.

The water goes off. She must crook her finger in a come-hither motion off-shot, because he creeps closer to her, close enough that the camera auto-focuses on her fingers as they wrap gently around his balls, then swiftly, very swiftly, on the head of his dick as it ascends toward the camera.

"Really," she says. She takes the camera out of his hand, cocking it at a weird angle as she kisses him and moves her hand from his cock to his face, caressing his stubbly cheeks. When he goes to kiss her thumb, she insistently shoves it in his mouth, making him whimper. She smiles.

"Shave first, will you? I'm still a little razor-burned from last night."

Her thumb traces a string of drool as it leaves his mouth; the camera goes on the counter as she plucks a towel from the rack and dries herself off. The camera's now at crotch level, showing his erect cock and her neatly trimmed pussy. He comes toward her and she pushes him gently away with a musical laugh.

"Come on," she purrs. "You're the one who wanted to make a porno movie. Shave that pretty face of yours and meet me in the bedroom."

"Yes, ma'am," he says.

She lifts the camera, points it at his face. He reddens, looks uncomfortable, then looks turned on.

"Yes, ma'am," she mimics. "I like that."

She doesn't turn the camera off as she goes into the bedroom. He races for the sink and there's the hiss of shaving cream. "Don't forget the lotion!" she calls as she lifts the camera and plays it first over a pair of black nightstands soiled with pooled candle wax and then over an incriminating trail—used condom, used condom, panties, boxers, tank top, his jeans, used condom (didn't this guy ever play basketball?), her jeans, one sock, another sock, her bra, a third sock, fuzzy yellow sweater, leather jacket, windbreaker; where the fuck was her other sock? She follows the trail lasciviously all the way back, still dripping a little. At the front door, where the jackets tangle like fucking snakes, she points the camera at herself, says, "Goddamn it, I'm a slut," and heads back to the bedroom, stopping at the bathroom door to point the camera at his ass while he shaves; he doesn't notice. She points the camera at her face, glowers fisheyed and whispers, "That's a pretty nice ass. Tastes good, too!" Then she returns to the bedroom and trains the camera over the ruined bed. The sheets crisp and white and dry twelve hours ago in anticipation of a seduction that turned them moist and wrinkled, covers bunched at the foot of it from where she'd kicked to get better purchase as she took him deep into her mouth, about two thirty, probably, or it might have been a little later. She sprawls on the bed and points the camera at her face.

She says with unassailable perkiness: "I don't know who you are, watching this, but my name is Rebecca Sinclair and I just fucked this guy, Brad, who I kinda barely know." She makes a show of being pensive. "He's a friend of my friend Sarah, but she really doesn't know him that well. This was our first date. It was kind of slutty of me." She cocks her head. "I just realized I don't remember his last name." She shrugs. "He told it to me, but"—smile, laugh—"I guess I just wasn't listening. God, I am such a cad. He was a pretty good lay, I guess. And now it's nine thirty in the morning, on Sunday, and I'm about to get some really"—here she rolls her eyes back and annunciates the word *ammmmAYzing* as clearly as it is possible to do so—"ammmm-mAYzing head, if last night is any indication." She cocks her head and smiles savagely. "And if not, I'm going to steal Brad's camera."

She shuts the LCD screen and guides the viewfinder to her eye, training it down her body as she begins to stroke herself casually, languidly, occasionally pausing to breathe into the microphone. She withdraws her fingers and holds them close to the lens, rubbing them together to demonstrate how wet she is. "You'd think I'd be tired," she purrs softly. "But I've been wanting more head since he finished the last round...I think it was about three thirty." She turns the camera and looks into it, making a show of whispering like she's telling a secret. "Even though the guy does need a shave. But we're taking care of that right now." She twirls the camera toward the bathroom, where the splashing of water can be heard, then back to her face. "I can't say I didn't plan this; I mean, there's the sweater"—she turns the camera searching unsuccessfully for it—"it's in the other room, I guess; I even"—the camera dips toward her trimmed pussy, whirring auto-focus on the landing strip—"trimmed for the occasion, which is sort of considered polite, I guess, though you wouldn't know it. It's so rare to find a guy who actually gives good head," she says, bringing the camera back up and looking into it bright eyed. "Usually it's like"—she pantomimes a halfhearted lick and fakes dull eyes and a stupid-person voice—"Okay, suck my cock now." She points the camera back at her crotch and begins masturbating, this time in earnest, her voice going quickly husky as she gets more into it. "I mean, don't get me wrong, I am an inveterate cocksucker, but...why am I telling you this? You're just a stupid camera. I am such a slut."

"Talking to yourself again?" She turns the camera toward Brad, who stands in the bedroom doorway. She trains the camera from his newly smooth face to his half-hard cock, which goes all the way hard as she lingers on it. When she returns the camera to his face, she can't tell if he looks embarrassed or pleased—but he started it.

"Again? No, actually, I was talking to you, fucker. Last night and now."

"I remember it being third person," he said. "*He's fucking me*, you know, *it's going in so deep*, et cetera."

She returns the camera to his cock. "You're the one who likes porn," she says. "I'm just doing the interview portion. So how long have you been a cock?"

She raises the camera to his face, which bears a blank expression. She turns the camera to her face again and says cheerfully, "I was just saying my name is Rebecca Sinclair, me and my twin sister just turned eighteen this morning, and we're about to fuck the football team. Yes," she says to Brad, "I've watched porn. Christ, what is this, the fifties?" Then she's facing the camera again: "Actually, my name is Rebecca Sinclair and I'm twenty-six and I'm about to get some amazing—*ammmmAYzing*—head from this guy named Brad"—she turns the camera to his face, the focus going blurry as he nears the bed—"who knows how to suck pussy like a champ."

"Champ?" he asks, feigning offense; she reaches for his hair, grabs and pulls. The camera goes spiraling crazily with the sound crackling under a sudden plaintive "Gaaaaah!" from its operator and a moment later it's pointing at the moist sheets while she moans.

"Yes," she says with an indecent tone to her voice. "Champ."

"I like that," he says, his words muffled wetly. "Champ."

It's a long few minutes of *click-whirr-whirr-whirr* as the camera sits there forgotten and Rebecca Sinclair moans. It's only when she tries to open her legs farther and coax him more completely onto the bed that she nudges it with her knee and says, "Oh yeah. We were making a porno."

She points the camera at her face, pink with lust and slack with pleasure. "See, Brad is giving me head right now," she says. With each moment she's having increasing trouble forming coherent words, and the camera's getting cocky as she pays less attention to it. "He's *eating* my fucking *pussy*," she says. "Like a...*ch-am-p*. He's giving me the most awesome...." She gasps and shivers. "Why isn't there a word for this? Guys can say…" Her mouth goes wide open; she's having trouble speaking. Her words come breathy and slow as Brad's mouth works on her succulently. "Guys can say, like, 'I got the best blow job,' but…there's no…equivalent—oh!—there's no equivalent term."

"Sure there is," says Brad, his words sounding distant, wet and muffled. "Tongue job. I'm giving you a tongue job."

"Fuck," she says thickly. "I actually like that. Tongue job. It sounds so…fucking…dirty…ah!"

Her eyes go fluttering closed, and when they open they're all unfocused, rolled back. She starts to drool a little. After a few long minutes of moaning and blinking, she points the camera closer, looking into its fish-eye, all bulging and distorted. "Brad should fucking teach a class on this," she says huskily, and points the camera down at him. Brad's smooth face is bobbing up and down between her splayed thighs, his tongue working eagerly. His face is wet, his chin and his cheeks slick with her, his mouth open wide as he licks her clit. He closes his mouth, puckered around her clitoris, and suckles as he licks her, which makes her gasp.

"Right there," she says breathlessly. "I like that. Sucking. Sucking is cool. Suck m—no, no, let's just call it a tongue job. That…is…very…good."

Her ass is lifted slightly off the bed, encouraged by his big hands cupped under it, squeezing slightly.

She keeps the camera trained on Brad as he alternately licks and sucks at her, alternating suck to lick and then doing both at the same time, which drives her crazy.

"God you look good between my legs, Brad," she mewls. "Doesn't he? Doesn't he fucking look good between my legs?"

She's talking in the third person again, which is exactly the same thing that happened the night before, spontaneously. She thought then and she thinks now that she is either an exhibitionist or a psychotic, maybe both.

"What's good about it?" asks Brad without ever taking his tongue far from her clit, which is its own kind of answer, but she talks just the same.

She brings the camera in close as he goes back to licking her. "First," she says tartly, "the fact that you even ask that is pretty fucking awesome. And second, you shaved when you were"— she's about to say "told to," but he chooses that moment to close his lips around her clit and suck gently, which was the first point she was going to make; the camera wobbles uncontrollably and she whimpers, "That," softly. "That's one thing, that little fucking sucking thing you do, where did you learn that? Fuck…"

He pauses just long enough to say, "I don't know," and she moans, "You're a good enough instructor—oh, fuck!—but better at the lab than the lecture." He goes back to sucking her clit. "But that's okay, I like the lab better than—fuck! That, that's point two, or three…fuck, fuck, fuck." He's stopped sucking and started licking, alternating quick up-and-down strokes with insistent circles that make her clit feel like it's at the bottommost point of a whirlpool, a sensation accented by the fact that he goes back to sucking a few minutes later, after the camera's gone careening around the bed a few times as her arms go all crazy. The auto-focus does not like this at all, but once the camera's on the pillow next to her, flecked with moisture, probably hers, possibly sweat, maybe drool, it's pointed at her face, off-center and mostly out of focus, but then it corrects itself and she stares into it.

She says urgently: "He keeps changing what he's doing, which usually annoys the fuck out of me, because most of the time you've got, like, half a minute of head so you have to make it work fast, but this guy, Brad, he's kind of into it." She searches for the words, eyes rolling back. "Brad, are you into it? You're not going to stop or anything are you?" He doesn't answer and her eyes go all the way back, making her look somewhere between an overacting porn star and Linda Blair in *The Exorcist.*

"Fucking camera," she says, and pushes it away violently, so that all it captures as the low-battery indicator begins to blink is the side of her rib cage, and the growing gap between her back and the moist sheets as she rises steadily against the strokes of Brad's tongue, rocking and moaning, five, ten, fifteen minutes of it as the battery light blinks URGENT, then CRITICAL, and the last things it captures is the crackling stream of profanities from her and the ferocious temblor of the bed as she seizes his hair and rides him, cursing till it all goes black, then bright again.

She's standing, camera on a table, the leading edge of a geology textbook beneath it; she corrects the camera's position, her yellow-sweatered breasts up close to the lens, nipples evident. She sits and regards the camera, looking sheepish.

"So," she says. "I'm not sure who you are, watching this, but you're definitely not Brad. I got my head, but I stole Brad's camera anyway." She cocks her head. "I guess that makes me a thief. You'd think he would have called me. I mean…to demand his camera back, if not for more sex. What an asshole." She leans close to the camera, whispering conspiratorially. "So…I just finished watching this tape, and"—her eyes roll—"wow. Brad. Kind of a dick, but…he did give some *really* good head. I am…"
She considers each word thoughtfully. "…*Extremely* turned on right now after watching that tape, the one and only porno I've ever starred in, up until about five minutes from now. My name is Rebecca Sinclair, I'm twenty-seven-years old, and about, oh, six weeks ago I met this guy Gabe, who is *awesome*. Anyway,

Gabe is an *ammmmAYzing* lay, like we are talking...the best. Fuck. Ever. But he says himself he's not so comfortable with the oral skills, and as you know that is *extremely* important to me; I am a cunnilingus queen...also a fellatio queen, but that's a different video. Anyway, no problem, Gabe says he wants to do it better, and I've got just the thing. I figure since dating politeness isn't dickwad Brad's strong suit...well, what am I talking about? I stole his fucking camera. I promise I won't steal your camera, Gabe. Probably. Anyway, wish me luck."

Off camera comes the sound of a door opening. "Talking to yourself again?" he asks.

She says musically, "No, actually, I'm talking to you, fucker." She turns the camera off.

THE GOTH CHICK

Lisette Ashton

I didn't see her at first. I only noticed the crowd standing around her. Seeing so many people gathered together—ignoring the pleasures of lounging by the pool or making their own entertainment on the nearby beach—I knew I had to see what was going on. The crowd was making enthusiastic sounds of shock and excitement that suggested something outrageous was occurring. I gave Rob a parting kiss on the cheek, told him to carry on working on his tan, and then eagerly elbowed my way through the throng to find out what was so interesting.

It was a swingers' weekend with more than a hundred couples in attendance at the resort. Lazy afternoon sunlight warmed the poolside and made the weekend seem idyllic. The scents of suntan lotion, sea breeze, and sex were constants in the air. Giggles, gasps, and groans provided a background of sounds that I knew I wouldn't find anywhere else. And I was curious to see what had captured the interest of so many people.

At such a large swingers' weekend, it wasn't surprising that someone had tried to do something out of the ordinary. The only real surprise was that someone had managed to do something that was so genuinely shocking it had garnered a crowd's interest. There were forty or fifty men and women gathered in a tight circle, away from the luxury of the pool and ignoring the charms of the beach.

A lot of the couples we'd hooked up with in the first day had been anxious to shock. Three of the women I'd danced with had confessed that they wanted to have more cock than anyone else at the party. Two of the guys I'd fucked each claimed they had the biggest cock. We swapped with one couple who wanted to organize the weekend's largest orgy, and I had feigned polite interest while talking to a woman called Stevie who said she wanted to eat every pussy at the party. Considering Stevie's tremendous ability to please with her mouth, I figured every woman at the party would be delighted to enjoy her skills. But her ambition seemed so mechanical I found it tiresome and unattractive.

Away from the swingers' party, in the sanctuaries of their separate suburbias, I didn't doubt every one of those outrageous couples would be viewed as daring trendsetters who boldly go where few other couples have gone before. But at a party with two hundred seasoned swingers, you have to be pretty extreme to get properly noticed. The large and enthusiastic crowd around the solitary woman told me that someone had finally done something to make everyone sit up and notice.

"Jesus!"

"I've never seen anything like it!"

"It's impressive. Impressive as hell! But what's the point?"

The voices around me only spurred my interest further. With renewed effort, I pushed my way between one couple and then said, "Excuse me," as I made my way through to the center of the crowd. A gap between couples allowed me a moment to see the attention-grabbing woman's face, and I was struck by instantaneous recognition.

I'd seen her before.

It was the goth chick.

Not that having seen her before was so remarkable. I was standing next to couples that I'd fucked the previous day. I saw Stevie: blonde and buxom and in the process of French-kissing a near-naked brunette. I was graced with a smile of recognition from the bee-stung pout of the redhead who had sucked Rob to climax immediately after that morning's breakfast. The redhead stood between two large, bronzed men, giggling demurely as each fondled her breasts. She wore bikini bottoms but they were pulled so tight I could see the shape of her pouting labia pressing at the thin fabric of the gusset. The crotch was dark with wetness. The redhead's name, I recollected, was Rebecca.

"Isn't she awesome?" Rebecca said, nodding toward the goth chick.

"I haven't seen her yet."

Rebecca giggled. "You're going to have to take a look."

The bronzed man to her right teased Rebecca's nipple between his thumb and forefinger. Kissing Rebecca's throat, he told her, "I hope you're not going to be as inaccessible."

Rebecca giggled and grabbed the hand at her breast. Easing his fingers away from her chest and guiding him down to her bikini pants, she allowed him to push his fingers deep inside. "You tell me," she breathed.

I was growing wet watching them. The shape of Rebecca's labia at the bikini's crotch was replaced by the thrust of his knuckles.

"Does that feel inaccessible?" Rebecca asked him.

It was tempting to just stand there and watch. I had earlier discovered that Rebecca was a natural exhibitionist. There was no worry in my mind that she would object to me standing and watching while she played with two men. In all honesty, I think she would have preferred to have had the attention of the entire crowd, but it seemed pretty clear that Rebecca wasn't going to get that much interest while all eyes were fixed on the goth chick.

"What's she done?" I asked. "Why is everyone looking at her?"

The bronzed man fingering Rebecca laughed and nodded toward the object of attention. "You'll have to look yourself." His voice was lazy with distraction and arousal. Rebecca shivered against him as he spoke. "You wouldn't believe us if we told you. And, if you did believe us, it would spoil the surprise."

I conceded this was fair advice, made my farewells with a "See you later," for all three of them, and then pushed back into the crowd to sate my curiosity. I was heading toward the female half of the goth couple who had arrived late yesterday evening. Rob had made some crass joke about the pair resembling Gomez and Morticia Addams but that association only made me feel more affection for them. I don't know many swinging couples who don't think of Gomez and Morticia as iconic role models. The characters were so openly sexual and publicly intimate that they always seemed to define the spirit of an open marriage.

The goth chick I had seen yesterday had been very little like the original Morticia Addams. Admittedly, her hair was jet black against alabaster skin, and her clothes were funereal in color. But her minidress was sexy and modern and short enough to show the crotch of her black lace panties, the neckline plunged so far down I guessed she was using sticky tape to keep some fabric discreetly concealing her boobs, and, unless she was attending the memorial service for a monochrome hooker, she looked as far from funereal as it was possible to get.

"I just don't believe what I've seen there."

"But what's the point?"

"Are you telling me you wouldn't want to see me like that?"

Frustration and anticipation built inside me as I caught snatches of conversation around me. Trying to ignore everyone else, focusing only on getting close enough to see, I barked a few more "Excuse me's" and finally found myself standing in front of the goth chick.

My pussy muscles clenched. The hot wet greed at the center of my sex struck with a breathtaking force.

The goth chick was still dressed in black. The color was strangely appropriate for her wan, porcelain flesh. Her hair was a lush and radiant jet that reflected the overhead lights as though the beams were dancing off polished chrome. The basque she now wore, cinched tight around a painfully thin waist, was an expensive combination of black lace and shiny black silk. The frilly suspenders protruding from the bottom of the basque were ebony: darkened as they stretched vertical lines across her whiter-than-white thighs toward her jet black stockings. But those details were only peripheral; exciting accoutrements that added to the most arousing aspect of the woman before me. The black heels, stockings, and basque were mere accessories that complemented the appearance of her pussy.

"What the fuck?"

The words came from the woman standing next to me. From the corner of my eyes I recognized Stevie. I figured she had finished with her brunette partner, pushed through the crowd in my wake, and gotten her first glimpse of the goth chick's exposed sex.

And I could understand Stevie's incredulous outburst.

The goth chick sat on a high-backed chair, her legs spread apart, revealing herself to everyone and anyone who cared to view her. And, even though Stevie had said the words, I had to admit the same exclamation was running through my mind.

"What the fuck has she done?" Stevie asked.

The goth chick turned her glance in our direction. She studied Stevie and asked, "Do you like it?"

I didn't give Stevie the chance to respond. Stepping forward, anxious and eager to get closer, I said, "I like it." I laughed and corrected myself and said, "No. I don't like it. I *love* it."

The goth chick's expression was haughty and almost superior. "Do you want to take a closer look?" She hooked her index finger into a beckoning claw and then pointed at the space between her spread legs.

I didn't bother to respond with words. Instead, to the approval of the onlookers, I got down on my knees and placed my face between her legs.

Someone wolf-whistled.

Someone else cried, "Go for it, girl!"

A few people started to applaud.

But I ignored all of them as I focused on the spectacle in front of me. I ignored every distraction as I tried to take in the sight of the goth chick's laced-up pussy.

We'd swapped with a goth couple once before two years earlier. They were new to the lifestyle, and Rob had responded to their "first-timer" ad because he was intrigued by the mention of her "intimate piercings." Of course, we'd encountered other couples with piercings through our journey in the swinging lifestyle. I'd even contemplated getting my nipples pierced until I heard that the healing time would mean my boobs would be a no-go zone for the best part of two months afterward. But the female half of the goth couple we hooked up with two years ago declared she had piercings in her clit and labia. And that had meant my interest was piqued, and I got my first encounter with ball closure rings beings used as body jewelry. Admittedly, that woman had been arousing, and the night we shared with them had been powerfully exciting. I think she and I licked each other to climax two or three times while Rob and her partner watched and wanked.

But that woman had not modified her piercings to the extreme of the goth chick in front of me. That woman had not replaced the BCRs of her piercings with a slim strip of leather. That woman had not laced her pierced labia so that her pussy was a tightly bound split of inaccessible flesh.

"Beautiful," I whispered.

"I know," the goth chick grinned.

I stared up at her from my position on the floor looking, I guessed, as though I was worshipping at her feet. I lowered my gaze from her large dark eyes and studied her sex with undisguised admiration. Her flesh was smooth and hairless. Through my experience in the lifestyle I had encountered shaved pussies before. But this one was so perfectly hairless I was instantly envious. There was no peppering of stubble—not even the suggestion of a follicle, or any blemish to indicate she had depilated or epilated or shaved—only silky smooth, sensual skin. The interlaced strip of leather, forming three bold black Xs down the length of her neatly sealed pussy was mesmerizing.

"Are you just going to look?" the goth chick asked.

I hesitated.

But only for a second. Moving my face forward, inhaling the sweet musk that emanated from the sealed split of her sex, I drew my tongue against her flesh.

The goth chick sighed.

It was all the encouragement I needed. I pushed my tongue more firmly against the lowest of the three black Xs and drew a line upward. I could feel the rough ridges of leather contrasting against the smooth flesh of her labia. The sensation was unreal and inordinately exciting. Growing giddy from the experience, I savored the sweet taste of her sweat and reveled in the sensation.

"Did you do this to yourself?" I murmured.

"My partner did it," the goth chick admitted. "Although I've been begging him to lace me up since we met."

I swallowed. The taste of her was on my lips and coating my tongue. Her sweat was as sweet as the richest balsamic; her musk was innately fresh and exciting. Each breath I took reminded me that her scent was filling my nostrils. I wanted to return my mouth to the sealed split of her sex but I resisted the temptation for a moment, savoring the pleasure of doing something so arousing and unusual.

"Why is it sealed? Do you like anal?"

She sniffed with disdain. "I don't do anal. That hole is one-way traffic only."

I was tempted to tell her that she was missing some of life's finest pleasures, but I knew this wasn't the place for such an argument. I lowered my face to her again, about to try another taste of her laced-up labia, and then paused. "Are you into sucking cock? Is that why you've done it?"

Her darkly painted lips sneered down at me. "I don't suck cock," she snapped haughtily. "What pleasure could I get from sucking a cock?"

It was clearly a rhetorical question. If she didn't know how much satisfaction a woman could get from chasing her tongue against a rigid erection, sucking it slowly to climax, and then tasting the explosion of satisfaction, I wasn't going to be able to convince her that it was worth trying. "I was just asking," I murmured. And, rather than trying to engage in further conversation, I placed my tongue back against the lowest X and began to slide it slowly upward.

The goth chick squirmed in her seat. Her tone was breathless as she hissed, "Higher. Do that a little higher."

Without rushing to obey, I traced my tongue over the middle X and then the uppermost. I allowed the tip of my tongue to ease against the tiny parting of the goth chick's flesh that wasn't contained behind the leather.

She moaned. "That's it," she mumbled. "Keep doing that."

I could feel the throb of her hidden clitoris beating from just below the surface. At the sides of my vision I could see her thighs growing tense. The definition of the muscles was vivid beneath the surface of her ultrawhite flesh.

"That's it," she insisted. "Keep doing that."

And I wanted to tell her that I had no intention of stopping just yet. The throb of her clitoris responded to my teasing. The pulse was solid and powerful, vibrating from her and making itself known to the tip of my inquisitive tongue. The bead of flesh was trapped just below the surface of her sealed pussy. I knew if I moved my face away and tried to study her sex, I wouldn't be able to see any symptoms of her pleasures. But I also knew if I continued teasing her with my tongue, I would soon be rewarded by the goth chick's orgasm.

"Go for it!"

"Make her scream."

I didn't need the words of encouragement from behind me to make me lap with more enthusiasm. I was already determined to wring an orgasm from the sealed lips of the goth chick's hole. But the cries of approval reminded me I was center stage, and the natural exhibitionist in me warmed to the idea that I was being watched and admired by the largest gathering of swingers that the weekend had seen so far. Buoyed by the idea of being admired, I danced the tip of my tongue against the goth chick's clitoris and basked in her sigh of satisfaction.

"Go on," she barked. "Keep doing that. Make me come." Her harsh tone was a spur to my excitement.

One of the most frustrating things about the lifestyle is that so many couples are polite and respectful. Occasionally I enjoy the thrill of being bullied and dominated. I adore being told to suck harder. I love being reminded that I'm a filthy bitch who worships cock or who loves the taste of pussy. Hearing the goth chick demand an orgasm appealed to my inner desire to be submissive.

"Get your tongue in there if you can," she gasped. "Lick my clit. Eat my cunt. Make me come."

My mouth was pressed tight against her. With every breath I was drinking the rich scent of her pussy and savoring the sweet, wet flavor of her excitement. I knew it would only take the pressure of a single finger against my own clit and I would orgasm. But that consideration seemed immaterial as I urged the goth chick closer to the point of climax. Trilling my tongue against her split, gasping as I felt the bead of flesh throb against my lips, I tore my mouth away as the Goth chick roared with satisfaction.

A handful of couples politely applauded.

Someone wolf-whistled again but the sound was easy to ignore. My head pounded with the need for satisfaction, and I was anxious to return to Rob so he could treat me to the climax my body needed.

"That was good," the Goth chick murmured. She reached down and stroked her fingers against my cheek. Her touch was sticky with a meld of perspiration and the dewy wetness she had ejaculated on my face. "Thanks," she added as an afterthought.

I was desperate to get back to Rob, but I also needed an answer from the goth chick about her remarkable appearance.

"Why have you done it?" I asked, nodding toward her laced-up pussy. "It looks beautiful. It's divine to play with. But isn't it frustrating for you?"

Her expression was inscrutable. "My partner and I came to an agreement," she began. Her voice was weary as though she had made this explanation so many times she was bored with the repetition. "I said I'd always wanted to experience a swingers' party. He said he'd always wanted to lace up my pussy with what he calls the ultimate chastity device. We decided to try each other's fantasies like this."

"But isn't it frustrating?" I asked again. "You clearly can't be penetrated. You don't do anal or oral. So, what are you getting out of it?"

For the first time since meeting her I heard the goth chick laugh. It was a melodic sound and would have been wonderful to share if I hadn't known she was laughing at me. I wanted to remind her that she couldn't enjoy the thrill of being penetrated by any of the male swingers at the party, and she was clearly missing an integral element of the experience.

But the Goth chick was no longer looking at me. She had hooked her finger into a beckoning claw and was gesturing for Stevie to take the place between her legs that I had occupied. Sparing me a final glance as Stevie began to nuzzle at the wet split of her laced-up pussy, her eyes glazing softly with the encroaching pleasure, the goth chick whispered, "I get enough out of the experience."

THE VITALITY OF YOUTH

Joanna Christine

Angela couldn't hear anything but the roar. The rain pounded down all around her. The roof over her head chimed a merry tune, and the wide floorboards of the porch were soaked. The trees whipped in the wind, bending under the weight, their leaves saturated with more rain than they could handle. She stood on the only part of the porch that had escaped the rain, but the mist of it still bounced up to caress her bare legs.

She watched it for a long time, content to let the pounding of the rain take the place of the thoughts that had run through her head ever since she had laid eyes on Jake.

Jake was long and lean, with hair a bit too long, a stride a bit too confident, and eyes that took in everything, whether you wanted to let him see it or not. His generous smile lit up a room and showed perfect teeth. He was handsome and he knew it.

He had come into her yard two months before with a business card and told her that he was looking for summer work on his break from college. As he told her how good he was at lawn work, she had been able to think of little else but how good he might be at other things.

She was thirty-eight, for crying out loud. Some would say that a man of twenty-one years old wasn't too young, but that didn't stop her from feeling like a cradle-robber. She was old enough to be his mother.

Angela sighed at the downpour, knowing it would now be several days before Jake came out to her house in his big truck with the trailer on the back. It would be days before she had another chance to watch from behind the curtains as he took a break from mowing the lawn and stripped off his shirt. She loved to move cautiously from room to room in her house, peering at him from the corners of her windows. Her favorite part was watching the muscles in his back work as he swept the weed-eater back and forth along the bottom of the hedge.

She thought he might have caught her once. She ducked behind the curtain as he turned her way, but she could have sworn she saw surprise in his eyes. When she looked back out, he was grinning down at the hedges—but when he came to the door for payment, she played it cool, offered him a glass of lemonade, and talked about nothing while they stood together on the porch, not touching at all. When he said good-bye and smiled at her, his attitude was completely respectful and she would have bought it, if not for that brief look in his eyes....

"You're imagining things," she told herself now.

She reached out into the rain, collecting the cool drops in her palm, letting them take a ticklish path down her arm before they dripped from her elbow. She found herself wondering how Jake's tongue would feel. She thought about it until her rational mind caught up with the daydreams, then she yanked her hand back, as if it were fire instead of rain falling from the sky.

The downpour went on for hours and never let up. The

gutters had long ago succumbed to the overload, and now sheets of water were falling merrily from every corner of her house. By the time night began to fall, the yard was saturated and puddles stood on either side of the driveway. It was still coming down when Angela turned off the lights and got comfortable on the couch, remote in hand.

She was flipping through channels when she heard the sound of tires on wet gravel. She looked out the window to see the shape of a long, black truck in her driveway. She watched for a moment, sure someone had simply lost his way—but then she saw a familiar silhouette climb out of the truck and start up the sidewalk. Her heart sped up as she watched Jake dash through the raindrops and toward her door. He had to knock twice before Angela shook herself out of her surprise.

When she opened the door, the sight that greeted her was better than any of her daydreams had been. Water dripped from his hair. His shirt was soaked, clinging, showing every long and lean muscle. He smiled that smile that said he knew damn good and well that he had no business being on her doorstep after the sun went down, but that he didn't care all that much for what was proper and what was not.

"Need a towel?" she asked. She was surprised to hear how deep her voice was. She sounded like a woman in heat.

Jake stepped into the house. He was a few inches taller than she was. He smelled like the rain and like some sort of cologne that seemed to make her knees a little shaky.

"I came by to tell you that I won't be able to mow your lawn tomorrow," he said.

They looked at each other. They both knew his visit had nothing to do with mowing the lawn. She wasn't stupid, and he wasn't blind.

"Let me get you that towel," she said. Neither of them moved.

They took their time looking each other over, openly saying with their eyes what they hadn't yet found the courage to say with their words. The rain poured outside the door and Jake dripped onto her hardwood. His smile slowly faded.

"I won't be able to mow anybody's lawn tomorrow," he said thoughtfully. "In fact, I doubt I will have much of anything to do for days."

Angela immediately thought of calling in sick to work. She nipped those thoughts right in the bud by pulling up her most obvious excuse. "I'm old enough to be your mother."

Jake smiled wickedly. "But you definitely are not." He reached out with one wet hand and touched her face. She was surprised by how forward he was. Shouldn't he be shy and sweet? Shouldn't she be the one doing the seducing, instead of the other way around? "I saw you looking at me," he murmured, and she blushed scarlet but refused to look away. "Since then, all I have thought about is kissing you."

His lips were wet. Water dripped from his hair as he kissed her. There was a puddle under her bare feet. It was ruining her floors. He was far too young for her.

She kissed him right back.

Before she had another chance to think about floors or towels or how young the young man was, he was kissing her in the middle of her living room and unbuttoning her shirt. His own clothes were soaked. Angela tugged on one dripping sleeve.

"We need to get you out of those before you catch cold," she said with a sanctimonious air.

"Yes, ma'am," Jake immediately replied.

He started with the shirt and worked his way down. Soon he was naked and his wet clothes were all over her clean floor. Angela let her eyes roam over him, and what she saw made her smile: he was obviously eager to please.

There was no place here for seduction or coy teasing. She knew exactly what she wanted, and she was sure he did, too. Within seconds she was on top of him on the couch.

Jake's hands were everywhere. He was eager but obviously not inexperienced—he paid attention to what she was doing and took his lead from there. Angela reached between them and stroked his cock before she sank down on it. He was bigger than she had thought he would be, and it actually hurt a bit when he slid all the way in. It had been way too long since she had done this. She rocked hard and then the pain was gone, replaced with nothing but pleasure.

Jake looked up at her as she rode him. The cockiness had been replaced with wide-eyed discovery. His hands clenched her hips. His mouth worked wonders on her nipples. Even as he lay there and let her do what she wanted, he was a willing participant. He had good staying power, too—Angela rode him for a long while before she got close, and he was right there with her the whole time.

Angela braced herself on his shoulders and ground down hard. She came with a primal growl. Jake held hard on to her hips and moved in short thrusts, helping her ride it out. He watched every move she made. Only when her orgasm was over did he thrust harder, pushing toward his own release.

"I'm going to come," he murmured, almost in apology, and she smiled down at him.

"Good."

She loved watching him as he came. His cock throbbed inside her and he thrust up hard, trying to get as deep as he could go. She watched him as the pleasure marked his handsome face. It went on a surprisingly long time, and when he finally relaxed and opened his eyes, he smiled up at her with that usual cocky grin. He was still rock hard inside her—the vitality of youth!

"Just how much of a man are you?" she asked as she sat there on him.

He smirked back at her. "I'll bet you know how to find out."

She started up his body. The wetness between them was slick and hot. She left a trail all the way up his chest, watching his face all the while. The expression in his eyes didn't change—he was just as excited as he had been when he first slid into her, and he wasn't looking to change his mind anytime soon.

He ran his hands along her thighs as she straddled him. His tongue was inside her before she had a chance to settle down where she had intended. Jake held her still so he could reach as deeply as possible. When that didn't get deep enough, he brought two of his fingers into play. Angela was shocked by how skilled he was—her assumptions about younger men were changing with every stroke of his tongue.

After that first eager taste, he slowed the pace, holding her hips tightly as his tongue set to exploring. He ran the tip of it over her lips, touching every inch, then slid up to her clit and teased around it, never quite touching where she really wanted, but leaving hints of how good it would feel when he finally did. He began drawing designs on her, and she tried to keep up with what they might be, but with every stroke of his tongue, her mind fell deeper into a haze of pleasure.

"Jake," she said, and tried to move, tried to get his tongue where she needed it most.

"Not yet," he murmured from between her thighs.

"Please."

He ignored her protests. "I love the way we taste," he said.

The thought that he could taste himself while he tasted her was enough to send her arousal to redline. Never in her life had she found a man who was willing to go down on her after he had come inside her, but Jake seemed to enjoy the act just as much as he had enjoyed fucking her.

He moaned as he licked and sucked her, and soon she was thrusting above him, grinding down, trying to get more pressure where she needed it. As pleasure began to edge into frustration, she grabbed his hair with both hands and guided his mouth there.

"Suck," she ordered. Jake chuckled and finally gave it to her, that deep and sweet sucking that sent her right over the edge. She cried out when she came.

Jake didn't stop. He pushed two fingers as deeply as he could and started to explore, looking for the places that would make her shudder and gasp. Once his fingertips swept over her cervix, and the pain-laced pleasure made her jerk hard in his arms. He sucked her clit into his mouth and stroked it with his tongue, long strokes that kept her right on the edge but didn't let her go over it. As she hovered there over his face, she realized that he was much more experienced than his tender age would lead a woman to believe.

He withheld her orgasm until she was trembling and begging. When she was right on the verge of collapse, he sucked hard and pumped his fingers in and out. She hovered on the edge for what seemed like forever, until she felt the slightest pressure of his teeth—not too hard, not too soft, silently demanding that she come. The shock of it was enough to send her over the edge with a loud and startled cry.

She collapsed over him. He lifted her with surprisingly powerful arms and flipped her underneath him. He slid his cock into her with one long thrust, and they both groaned. "Is there anything you won't do?" she asked, still trying to catch her breath.

"I haven't found anything yet," he answered.

"What do you taste like?" she asked. In response, he kissed her. She tasted the familiar taste of herself and there was something else there, something deeper and saltier. Angela knew that must be him, and she was immediately ready for another round. She bucked up into him and he grinned down into her eyes.

"I hope you have some sick days saved up at work," he said.

Angela laughed. She hoped it would rain all week.

CUNNILINGUS 101

Rachel Kramer Bussel

Counting the minutes ticking by on the overhead clock, Rick shifted in his seat at the very back of the eight-hundred-seat lecture hall, idly flipping the pages of his *Econ 101* textbook as Professor Vanderbilt droned on at the front of the class. The pompous, balding, tenured professor acted as if they should be honored to have him even set foot in front of them, let alone actually teach them something.

Who really cares about supply and demand, anyway? Rick thought.

He was eighteen, and still adjusting to campus life. Berkeley, California, was a hell of a lot different from his hometown in rural Virginia—just as he'd desired. If he really thought about it, he could cast his mind back to a time when his parents' house, with its huge backyard, rec room, cable TV, and unlimited goodies in the fridge, contained all he'd ever really needed, but now that all seemed like another era, or another person's life—pre-porn, pre-erections, pre-fantasies, pre-sex. He considered himself barely beyond virginity, and he wondered if there should be some qualifying test to pass, with losers sent back for remedial sex training. He knew he'd yet to truly taste the pleasures of female flesh, but he was sure he'd come up a winner once he got the chance. In Rick's mind, he was a cocksman par excellence.

He'd always known he was smart enough to go to a school like Cal, and in fact schoolwork was proving much easier than he'd expected. It was still a challenge, but if he kept up with the reading and diligently studied every afternoon, he seemed likely to coast through his first semester with excellent grades. But even at such a liberal school, where there were classes on porn that his fellow students clamored to get into, plus parties galore, if you knew where to look, Rick was aware of some things that simply couldn't be taught—at least in a lecture hall. Things like how to calm the raging erections he found himself sprouting during class when the hot girls showed up in skimpy tank tops, tossing their silky hair to the left and then the right, lifting it up and piling it on top of their heads with a barrette. Things like how to actually speak to a pretty girl, rather than just stammering stupidly. Things like how to woo two girls into his bed at once, like his buddy Kevin, whom he'd seen walking around with a blonde and a redhead, both sexy as could be, strolling the campus as if all he needed was a brunette to complete his fantasy.

There was one girl in class, Eliza, who simply mesmerized him. She wasn't necessarily the hottest girl, or the one with the biggest boobs or the prettiest smile. She wasn't nearly as flashy as some of the other women he went to school with, but something about her, from her old-fashioned name to the things she wore (little cardigans decorated with flowers or sparkly bits that always caught the sun) to the way she held her pen, her fingers resting atop its length as opposed to wrapped around it like everyone else (yes, he'd noticed even that), made him want to talk to her. Okay, truth be told, he wanted to do more than simply talk. He wanted to kiss her all over, taste every inch of her beautiful skin. Most of all, he wanted to lick her pussy until she screamed. Until she came all over him. Until she went absolutely, completely, totally wild. Until she told him she'd never been with anyone who could make her climax so hard. Until she begged him to do it again.

That's what Rick thought about as Professor Vanderbilt wrote on the board and walked them through hypothetical problems they'd encounter running their own company. The only business he wanted to start, or be part of, was one that taught guys how to really eat pussy. Even thinking of those words—*eat* and *pussy*—gave him an instant hard-on. Rick shifted in his seat as his eyes swept along Eliza's back, hunched over as she doodled in her notebook. He'd lucked out with a seat near hers, but across the aisle, so that he was free to observe her unnoticed.

It wasn't that he hadn't been with girls before. Even in his sleepy small town, there'd been plenty of opportunities for sex. Marta had "made him a man," as his best friend Kyle would say, one day in a pile of leaves in a deserted park on their way home from school. Sex with her had been fun, but he'd been so nervous that he could barely enjoy it. She'd let him fuck her, but had balked when he'd asked her to spread her legs for him so he could taste her. Apparently, in his town, nice girls didn't do that—even when they were asked by sweet boys who'd just offered up their virginity.

His only other experience with a mouthful of girl parts was with Katie, who'd pressed his face against her sex and ground herself into him through the thin layer of her panties. He'd been able to taste her unique flavor through the cotton, but it had been so brief, just a tease. He'd wanted her to relax, let him savor the experience and gently peel down her undies to reveal the treasure beneath, but she'd been so demanding, pressing and slamming and shoving against his eager-to-please tongue, that he didn't know how to tell her to slow down, nor did he ask her to remove the flimsy but still pesky panty barrier. Before he knew it, she was dragging him up by his hair, kissing his lips, pushing her wet panties aside, and guiding his cock inside her.

Rick had come to Berkeley ready to find a girl who'd want him for more than just momentary pleasures, though the idea made him nervous. A real girlfriend would expect more from him than a cursory lick and pinch of her clit. She'd want him to get down there and stay until he could prove he knew what he was doing. And even more than wanting the rapture of seeing a girl's pretty lips wrapped around his dick, like he'd seen in the porn movies that his suitemates frequently watched on their communal TV, he wanted to make a girl come with just his lips and tongue. He wanted to feel her wetness rubbing against him, taste her juices, hear her moans.

As it turned out, Eliza was the one who approached him, that very day in economics class. She stood in front of his desk as he gathered up his belongings, giving him a start when he realized that the girl of his dirty dreams was right in front of him.

"Hi—Rick, right?" she asked, then licked her lips, fidgeting from one side to the other. Her hair, held back by barrettes with butterflies on them, stayed in place, but he noticed a slight bounce to her breasts. "I wanted to see if you'd like to be study partners. Vanderbilt suggested to me during office hours that I find someone and, well, I thought you might need some help in here too." She looked at him with wide, hopeful eyes, eager for his approval. He stared back, trying to see if she meant more than simply mastering means and medians and stock market prices. He wasn't sure, but his cock seemed to answer for him, surging upward in his pants.

"Yeah, that'd be great."

"What about tonight?" she asked, then looked away, as if she regretted sounding too eager.

"Tonight's fabulous," Rick told her, both because he'd get to see her sooner and because his roommate would be out until at least one in the morning at some fraternity function. He waited until they'd exchanged numbers and he'd given her his address to let his mind slip back to fantasyland, where Eliza was on her back on his bed while he held her legs apart and dove between them. His mouth watered, as if he could already taste her. He glanced up to see her walk out the door, and wondered what kind of underwear—if any—she sported beneath her tight skirt. Rick looked around and noted that he was the last student remaining in the large classroom.

When she arrived at his place later that evening, Rick thought he was ready. He'd done his best to decorate his meager apartment. He'd wanted her to notice, but she barged past him right into his bedroom.

"We can study later," she said, her body poised to give him the most advantageous view of her breasts, no longer covered in a sweater, but now in a simple white button-down top that strained against her chest. She cast him a beguiling look, and he realized she didn't have to notice a damn thing about their surroundings, as long as she was ready for him. This was more than he could've hoped for, and it felt perfect. Maybe she'd been dreaming of the same thing he had all along.

"Rick, I—" she stammered then, and he smiled. She was just as nervous as he was, and he no longer worried that she'd attack him, devour him even as he tried to devour her. She wanted him, the real him, not some fictional superhero he-man. She undressed slowly, her eyes remaining locked on his even as her fingers nimbly unbuttoned and unzipped, her movements sly and sensual, until she lay there before him, totally naked, waiting, wanting.

As Eliza lay on her back, Rick dove in. At first, he barely tasted a thing, because he was moving so fast. It was as if he was swimming, kicking his legs slightly in time to his mouth's actions, while his fingers laid her open, trying to make up for lost lessons, cram semesters into minutes, as he sought her sweet spots. She didn't sit up and lecture him, pointing to where their bodies joined to demonstrate what she wanted. No, instead, Eliza, ever the English major, showed but didn't tell. She gently lifted her hips when she wanted Rick to move lower, and held open her hood when she wanted him to attack her clit. When he was doing something right, she yelled and moaned and banged her fists on the bed, a powerful signal. Eliza moved her hips in circles at one point, and he got it, moving his tongue in corresponding circles in the other direction.

And somewhere along the way, Rick did indeed become the cocksman—and the tonguesman—of his biggest fantasies. He earned an *A+* in attention to pussy detail as he licked his wide, long, warm, soft, strong tongue from the very base of Eliza's slit all the way on up, then curled it into a point and teased her clit until she groaned. He ran his fingers all over her skin, up and down her legs, then pinching along her inner thighs, all the while getting the entire lower half of his face smeared with her juices. When his tongue was completely buried inside her, his nose smashed up against her mons, he reached up to pinch those pretty little nipples he'd seen straining against the thin bras and tank tops she kept them wrapped up in during class. He even added a finger inside her, wriggling it alongside his buried tongue.

He was a natural, and his learning curve was short and fun to ride. When she finally managed to push his head aside, they were both overwhelmed by what had passed between them. By then, he didn't even want to fuck her, but preferred to wait, wrapping her fingers around his cock for a few quick pumps before coming in a geyser of hot semen. Eliza fell asleep soon and Rick just looked at her naked body in repose, so lush and gorgeous, so much more than he ever could have hoped for in class.

Weeks later, again feeling bored in Professor Vanderbilt's class, he took a moment to think about Eliza's beloved pussy, the one he now got to taste every single day, often several times. No matter how his official report card turned out, he'd mastered the most important lesson of all—but that didn't mean he'd stopped trying to learn. *Far from it,* Rick thought, as he patted the small egg vibrator tucked in his pocket. He planned to surprise Eliza with it while he licked her to ecstasy later that night, and could practically feel the vibrations ripping through her already and hear her moans of bliss.

Letting the professor's words travel over him, he stared at Eliza's back, thought of her tasty cunt, and looked forward to earning his extra credit in Cunnilingus 101.

READ HER LIPS

Stan Kent

I was between relationships, like that platinum card world traveler who is always between flights, never home long enough to call a place home; in matters of the heart and parts lower down, a temporary resident of that limbo-land where it is too soon to get involved with someone else because you're still not over the last paramour. In other words, my life sucked. I was one of the walking wanking wounded; of all the things that the losing of love dumps on your parade, the worst is the sudden departure of regular, convenient sex. I was deep in the solitary confines of carnal withdrawal, but as I hit bottom, I resolved not to let my being unlucky in love cause me to sit in my newly rented, boxes unpacked apartment moping and celibate. No way. Hollywood and all of its diversions and perversions beckoned. I may not have been ready for a relationship, but I was not opposed to an uncomplicated quick fuck to get me back in the saddle.

I drifted from bar to bar, club to club, house party to house party, book signing to book signing, and that final stop for the truly desperate: no, not strip clubs, but literary get-togethers. At several of these torturous events I spied a stunning redhead. She had a dirty laugh and sense of humor to match. She swore with the perverted panache of a character in a Henry Miller novel. She held a beer bottle like it was a cock and drank booze like she was making up for all the people in AA. She had muscles in all the right places and wore clothes that showcased her fit physique. I wanted her more than a dog drools over a juicy bone.

Leesa (that was how her name was spelled and pronounced, often drawn out like she was being announced—"Here's Leeeeeeeesa!") was, as I soon found out, also a lesbian, but that didn't stop us from becoming overnight best friends. She was on the rebound just like me. We were immediately part- ners-in-crime, fellow travelers on a journey to rehabilitate our love and lust lives. If the universe was fucking with me as some kind of karmic payback for my breakup, then at least it had a perverse sense of humor. Oh, the escapades we enjoyed. They were too numerous to mention, but let's just say Leesa had more balls than David Beckham has bend. I once watched in shock and awe from the passenger seat as she talked herself out of a major traffic ticket for an illegal turn and a certain DUI with quite an assortment of forbidden substances in the glove box by asking the cop out for a date. It worked. I will not even bother to describe the incident with the baseball bat, that to this very day I still keep in my car, not so much for protection, but for the memories it brings.

We cruised parties. We were each other's pimps, surveying the bodies, often hitting on two girls together—one for her, one for me. As a consequence of our friendship, I spent more time in lesbian bars than Rosie O'Donnell. If a fag hag is a woman who hangs around gay men then I was a dyke tyke.

There was a sexual tension between us but never a question that we would become lovers. We were like brother and sister, God and Satan, yin and yang, a role-reversed Will and Grace, but really cool and nowhere near as annoying. Together we completed each other, filling the voids left by our previous romances, healing the hurts with a carnally celibate camaraderie until the real thing came along.

After one particularly drunken night that involved us getting thrown out of a crashed wedding party at a fancy hotel, we woke up in the late afternoon in the same bed. Yes, we sometimes slept together, sometimes naked, but again, there was no sex. We'd missed breakfast and lunch, so we went for an early dinner at our local Italian restaurant—the Fart—Farfalla to be exact, and yes, did I forget to mention that we lived on the same street a few buildings from each other? That's how fated we were to be friends. The commonalities were amazing; she was also trying to be an author while holding down another job. Through my day job, I even knew her uncle who I had no idea was her uncle until we happened to run into him at a restaurant in what turned out to be a farcical scene straight out of a French movie. The look on his face was priceless as he looked from Leesa to me to Leesa as we looked up from our drinks and said his name in stereo. After that we often joked that we were terrible twins separated at birth.

Back to the Fart, where the terrible twins were eyeing a tasty new waitress who as the flying fickle finger of fuck fate would have it was our server for the night. Her name was Azalea, and she was an exotic bloom worthy of her moniker. She looked part Japanese, part European, with long flowing black hair framing a tight little body that was bursting out of a too-tight tuxedo shirt. Her boobs and buns begged for a squeezing. Her smile cried out for kissing. Her pussy, I presumed, demanded a regular and hearty fucking.

As we ogled Azalea, Leesa leaned over to me and whispered in my ear as Azalea took care of the table next to ours. Leesa, as it turned out, not only knew her women but her flowers, too. "Azalea signifies first love. Maybe this is the one, Stan. Maybe this is the one that'll be your first love since your breakup." "I like it. She is gorgeous."

As Azalea turned to leave the table, Leesa rushed in where the timid would have stuttered and sputtered. If Cupid used a bow and arrow, Leesa came armed with an Exocet missile.

"Hey, Azalea, would you go out with my friend? He thinks you're gorgeous. You'd look good together. He is really cool, and from what I hear, totally hot in bed."

I didn't have time to be embarrassed, and by now I was used to Leesa's no-bullshit manner.

Azalea appraised me with seductive eyes. I raised my glass. She nodded and turned to Leesa and performed a similar appraisal before saying, "I'm sure he is very cool and a great fuck while still being very nice, but no thanks, I have a boyfriend, but I *will* go out with *you*. We have an agreement. I can have as many girlfriends as I like, and I'd like to have you."

As Leesa's partner-in-crime, this was an occupational hazard for me, and I really wasn't that bummed to be the third wheel on this bi-cycle. That Leesa was going to get some made me feel good, goddamnit. The universe was fucking with me.

The rest of the evening was spent flirting and drinking, and when Azalea got off there was much more drinking, and then we stumbled to my apartment, which was the closest of our respective pads, and absinthe ensued and somewhere in there the green fairies materialized and we were all decamped on my futon, enjoying the buzz. Azalea was in the middle. Candlelight flickered, shadows darted around the room, and Leesa's tongue likewise flickered and darted in and out of Azalea's mouth. The futon was small, a quick post-breakup purchase to begin my new life, and what a christening it was receiving. Leesa and Azalea acted as if I wasn't there. I was like a pillow that they pressed up against.

Azalea even dug her hand into my arm as Leesa slid her hand down Azalea's jeans and into her pussy. Watching the rippling of Leesa's fingers underneath the cloth was captivating. They were so into each other they didn't mind me staring. I was hard enough to burst but I couldn't join in. This was Leesa's scene and Azalea had made it very clear throughout the evening that dick was off limits. If I'd whipped it out, I knew that would have spoiled things for Leesa, so I lay there reincarnated as a lucky pillow to be enjoying the feel, sights, and sounds of Azalea and Leesa getting it on. Every muscle twitch and writhe played through my body. Every pornographic visual fed my voyeur's cravings. Every sound tickled my ears and fancy. I stayed Zen and distant and not frustrated by telling myself I was an orgasmic observer whose job it was to document everything because this was one epic erotic story that had to be told, and I am a writer of epic erotic stories, and I was lucky enough to have two muses inspiring me, and well, here we are.

Leesa was naked, having disrobed like her clothes were on fire. She likewise incinerated Azalea's jeans, tugged down her panties, popped the buttons off her shirt as she tore it open and squeezed her bullet-hard nipples before diving between Azalea's widespread legs, the right one of which was wrapped around my leg. There were times as Azalea flexed her leg that her thigh rubbed across my crotch, and yes, I cop to the fact that I maneuvered myself into a position that facilitated such "accidental" contact. It wouldn't take much to make me come in my pants. This scene was scorching, blazing, inferno hot, their bodies fits together so well, their soft skin blended into a gorgeous canvas, their arms entwined, they flowed and merged as they made the beast with two backs, becoming one and then two and back to one as they slipped over and around each other.

Leesa had tongue-walked up from Azalea's cunt to do some major macking on Azalea's upper lips and then eventually tongue-walked back down to lap away between her thighs. Leesa's licking rose above the Enigma "Principles of Lust" that I'd put on the CD player to loop endlessly, appropriately. Azalea mewled these delightful little sighs punctuated with desperate gasps as Leesa drove her over the edge. Together they were a perfect sexual symphony that my heavy breathing complemented.

Leesa came up for air and our eyes made contact as she kissed Azalea, whose juices now painted Leesa's face. Azalea broke from the kiss, her tongue slipping from Leesa's to lick her clean. It was a tender, sexy moment that I felt truly privileged to witness. I'm not at all religious, but let me tell you, this was a holy moment.

Leesa nibbled on Azalea's neck, and floating out of Enigma's audio porn I made out a little whispering, a few giggles, and then they both turned to me. They were in a totally blissed out post-fuck state. Their eyes were glazed, but Leesa's glistened with a wicked intent as she said, "How would you like to learn to eat pussy from a lesbian so that when you get a new girlfriend she'll be your fuckslave forever?"

I honestly don't remember what I said in reply, but my answer was never in doubt as every synapse in my brain and every nerve in my body screamed, "FUCK YES." The room spun faster than my world turned, and it wasn't the absinthe giving me vertigo. It was all I could do to hold on.

And hold on I did as I joined Leesa between Azalea's dripping thighs.

Leesa maneuvered a candle closer and out of the shadows

emerged Azalea's pussy. Her labia were parted and the pinkness glistened. Her clitoris was swollen, and I swear it was beating like a tiny heart. Leesa motioned me to join her for a close-up. Our faces pressed together. I felt her hot breath bounce back from Azalea's flesh. It was like we were kids defying a parental lights-out edict, reading a hard-to-put-down book by whatever illicit illumination we could get our eager hands on.

"Go ahead, show me what you've got," Leesa said.

I felt suddenly very self-conscious, but the scent of Azalea's sex was irresistible. I put out my tongue and licked from that tender space just below her pussy and above her ass upward until I flicked her clitoris. It was beating a tattoo. She shuddered. I felt good.

"You're going too fast. Slow down. Tease her."

I mumbled something to be agreeable but it was not wise to speak when drinking from the fount of Venus. Azalea twitched, but not in good way.

"Be careful. Don't blow on it."

I backed away.

"I wasn't. I know that much. It's hard to concentrate with you giving me a running critique."

"Well, how else are you going to learn? Here, let me show you."

I backed away slightly. Leesa hovered like a hummingbird a few inches from Azalea's parted, flowering cunt. She spoke softly.

"You have to read her lips. It's called cunnilingus and there's more to that old joke about being a cunning linguist. It's true. Her pussy will tell you what she wants if you learn its language. All pussies are different and what works with one might not work with another. The only way you'll figure it out is if you learn to speak fluent twat by reading her lips. It also helps when it's shaved and doesn't tickle you as much. You can see so much more. Look how it's parted, how her flesh arranges itself. You have to get to know it. You have to leaf through her lips with your tongue, like this."

This monologue was an eye-opener. I'd gone down and loved going down and never really received any complaints, but I'd never thought of it in such individual terms. I treated pretty much every cunt the same, and for the first time I realized how wrong that was. When all you've got is a hammer then everything looks like a nail, and as Leesa's tongue coaxed Azalea's pussy alive, exploring the folds, I suddenly understood how to speak fluent twat. There weren't just nails to be hammered but screws and fasteners and hooks and eyes and staples and glue and this analogy just ran out of steam, but Leesa's leafing through a book was a good analogy full of express train steam from the days when they had such locomotives. Azalea's body responded to Leesa's mouth, her cunt dancing with Leesa's tongue like they were skilled ballroom partners with a natural, primal connection.

Leesa backed away. Azalea raised her ass. Leesa spoke and we were so close I felt the words.

"She'll tell you with her body what she likes and what she doesn't. You just have to learn to read her lips and slow down, and don't be too light and be careful with the biting, and when you get real comfortable, and are communicating on the same wavelength, you can do this."

Leesa turned her head slightly sideways and opened wide, taking all of Azalea's cunt into her mouth, sucking her labia like she was taking a bite of juicy, tropical fruit. She backed away, releasing the labia with a slurp as her tongue beat on Azalea's clitoris. Leesa took my finger with hers and slid them into Azalea's pussy, guiding me to her G-spot like she knew the way by heart.

We massaged the tender flesh, pressing her clit into Leesa's lips. Azalea thrashed. Leesa grabbed one leg and I grabbed the other. Leesa pulled her mouth away and nudged me forward, whispering in my ear, "Wear her like a pair of sunglasses."

I wrapped my arms around Azalea's thighs and pulled her ass upward, arching her body. Following Leesa's example, I opened wide and took Azalea's sex into my mouth, closing my lips around hers. My tongue traversed the folds of her flesh, up and down, side to side, as I read her lips. Leesa was right, they did guide me. I pulled back, but didn't release cleanly; by design, by intent, I nipped at her skin just before latching on to her clit the way countless women before had sucked on my cock.

There's a scene in *Blade Runner* where Harrison Ford fights one of the replicants played by a totally sexed-out Darryl Hannah. She clasps her thighs around his head and is squeezing the life out of him but he breaks free and shoots her and she goes into this frenetic seizure on the floor, all limbs pounding and head shaking and screaming.

That was Azalea as she came. She squirted, soaking me and my futon. I sputtered and gasped for breath, realizing in the midst of it all that I had rubbed myself off in my pants from all my squirming on the futon. I was a sticky, happy, and totally smug mess. Azalea was lost to the world, legs splayed, small breasts heaving, her hands covering her face. It looked like she'd stuffed her fingers in her mouth to stifle her screams. She was alive but in an altered state.

Leesa turned to me.

"Congratulations, you'd make a good lesbian."

"Thank you."

"I mean it. Someday you're going to make some lucky hetero chick very happy."

Never a truer word was spoken, from any set of lips. Thanks

to Leesa I've become a connoisseur of cunt fluent in all the major dialects, but I'm always learning and discovering new things by keeping an open mind between an open pair of legs, and always, always, taking the time to read her lips.

Thanks Leesa, and thanks Azalea. If ever you ditch that boyfriend, you know who to call.

DOWN THERE

Julia Moore

All right, I'll be honest. I have never had any idea of what's going on down there. None whatsoever. This won't come as a total surprise to anyone who knows me. I may very well one day win the prize as the person with the worst sense of direction in the entire world. Spin me around twice and I can't tell you which way I started. Ask me where North is, and you'll get a blank stare. In Paris, I couldn't find the Eiffel Tower. In London, I never saw the Thames. In the one-horse town where I grew up, I couldn't give directions to Main Street.

But still—shouldn't I have at least had a *concept* about the map of supposed pleasure situated between my legs? Shouldn't I, when asked in a husky whisper, have been able to direct a wayward traveler past the gates of my outer lips toward that central circle, that bull's-eye located in the middle?

Unfortunately, no.

My sense of direction was even worse than usual in bedroom circumstances. As I had no idea how to reach that faraway place called "coming," I couldn't help a stranded wanderer. Like a tourist vainly in search of an elusive vision, I never experienced anything to write home about.

Knowing my history, you won't be shocked to learn that I paired myself with a partner who couldn't bring it upon herself to ask for directions. On this side of the ring, we had Ms. Know-It-All, so vainly secure in herself that she was rendered unable to admit to being lost. And on my side, we had a befuddled girl who had gone so completely astray that she wasn't even facing the right direction in the ring. Instead, she stared confusedly out at the audience, as if someone—*anyone*—might see the need in her eyes and offer genuine and helpful assistance.

"See, Miss? Your clit is right here. And if you rub it like this, just a soft little tickling touch...a whisper caress...then you'll come. Oh, how you'll come—"

I imagined something like that happening to me. With the right teacher, I'd be able to learn, wouldn't I? Even those with the worst sense of direction can follow a map after repeated instruction, no matter how painful the process. Unfortunately, Tracey wasn't the right teacher. Or I wasn't the proper pupil. For whatever the reasons, we were woefully mismatched. Yes, she was butch and I was femme, but those two definitions don't equate instant success between the sheets. Just because a girl wears a wallet chain and a wife-beater T-shirt doesn't mean she can make a pretty lipstick lesbian like me purr like a cat in heat.

Occasionally, I tried to touch myself solo and reach those magic heights I'd heard of from friends. But even though I used my fingers, a bottle of expensive lube, and a slick little pink toy with a motor inside, I never seemed to even get close. With Tracey I felt almost nothing—and this started to make me believe I was destined to be a failure between the sheets. There are people who hate to travel. They get nothing out of the experience of seeing distant lands. They feel distaste upon entering an airport and have no joy when they cradle a passport. I was starting to feel like that—except I felt that way in bed. Romantic candles made me nervous. Pretty nighties left me feeling like a fraud.

So I said good-bye to Tracey, hoping that if I left a bad situation, a good one might come my way. It wasn't necessarily up to me to locate the right woman, was it? Some lucky people are simply in the right place at the right time. They don't have to travel to far-off lands in order to experience the thrill of the new. New can be right there—on your block, or at your office.

But new was scary.

When I went on dates with the butch types who tend to ask me out, invariably they'd quiz me in their seductive bedroom talk, trying to uncover what I liked. The truth was that I didn't know. I became hypersensitive, and very worried, and that combination did not prove to be the perfect recipe for sexual sparks with any of my potential mates.

That's when I met Nicole. Nic was totally different from Tracey. Totally different, in fact, from any woman I'd ever met. She had a job in the same building where I worked, and we began to run into each other on a daily basis. Sometimes, I'd be on the wrong floor, or suddenly realizing I'd taken a left at the last cubicle instead of a right, and that's precisely when I'd see her, as if she might have taken a wrong turn, as well. Or as if she'd taken a correct turn, and that turn had led her to me. She'd wink at me, or wave, and then head wherever she was going, and I would stare after her, longingly, wondering what it would feel like to always know you were headed in the right direction.

Other times, we'd both pull into the underground parking structure at the same instant, and I'd tail her fine ass to the elevators, so that I wouldn't get lost in the maze below street level. She never commented on my footsteps behind her, but when she'd turn to look at me, her dark eyebrows would go up and she would smile.

I heard several of the other local lesbians talk about her in the office: Nicole. Nikki. Nic. They sighed when they said any variation on her name, discussing her bountiful good qualities. Aside from the fact that she wore faded 501s as if they'd been made for her body, she was a winner. Nic never got upset with work crises, never appeared put out or perturbed by any of the daily dysfunctions occurring in the office. She had a way about her, an ease, and I started to imagine her when I touched myself in my nightly attempts to reach that distant shore. I thought about Nicole with her firm hand on mine and her steady, calm attitude, showing me the way, leading me home.

Then one rainy Sunday, we ran into each other away from the office, at a fancy gourmet market on the outskirts of Beverly Hills. This was my favorite store to shop in because it was so small. I never wandered away from my basket only to find that I had no idea which aisle it was on—or which aisle *I* was on. I liked how the shelves were low, so you could see over them and view the entire layout of the store. It was as if the place had been built with someone like me in mind. So I was off in my own world, when Nicole came up behind me.

"Hey," she said.

"Hey—" I turned to look at her. "Hey" was our standard greeting.

"We meet again."

I nodded and smiled.

"Do you know where they keep the liquor here?"

Someone asking me for directions! That was a first. And a butch girl admitting that she didn't know where something was—hell, that was a startling new experience after being with Tracey. I took in the carefree attitude she seemed to exude. She had on casual clothes: jeans, a T-shirt, cool shoes. Her shades were up on her thick dark-brown hair, and she had a little half smile that made me bite my lip, wondering if she could tell that I found her attractive.

"I'm going that way," I told her, and led her to the liquor aisle. Oh, did I feel in charge. I was showing someone else where something was! I watched as she perused the shelf, then chose an expensive bottle of single-malt.

"Party?" I asked.

"Of one," she told me.

"But you're buying the good stuff."

"I'm worth it," she said, shooting me that sexy grin again, and I found myself giggling, girlish. And I also found that my panties felt suddenly damp in the center. I was very aware of the region between my legs—as if a beacon had been lit, sending out shivers of light across the sky, heralding the existence of a hot new nightspot in town.

"And you?" she asked, looking over my basket. I had grapes, cheese, and crackers, and I had been on the way to the wines when she stopped me. On my own, without Tracey the know-it-all to coach me, or any one of my useless dates, I'd been slowly enjoying the freedom to choose my own brands and even learn my own tastes.

Now, I said, "What about a party of two?" I couldn't believe the words were coming from my mouth, but I was pleased that Nicole didn't seem surprised in the least.

"Sounds perfect," she said, lifting the basket from my hand. As we headed toward the checkout counter together, she said, "I've seen you all over the office, but we've never really been properly introduced. My name's Nicole." *I know,* I thought, but didn't say out loud. Oh, yeah, I knew exactly who she was. Instead, I said, "Cat. Catalina, actually."

"I love that place," she told me.

"So did my parents," I said, not wanting to admit that the one time I'd attempted to go there myself, I'd gotten so hopelessly turned around I'd missed the ferryboat and wound up canceling the trip entirely.

"I live on Rose Boulevard," she said. "Do you know where that is?"

I shook my head. I didn't want to tell her yet that I didn't know where anything was.

"Just east of Fairfax. Not as far as La Brea."

East, I thought. Away from the ocean. I'd learned that much. But which way was east from where we were? With the rain, I couldn't even rely on which way the sun was setting....

"You want to follow me?"

Now I nodded, and after paying for the groceries, I trailed after her back to her apartment, nerves throbbing with worry that I'd lose her on the way, but it was as if I'd suddenly transformed into one of those people who always knows where she's going. The kind of person who claims to have "metal" in her head. That was me. I made it following behind her easily, and pulled right into the space next to hers. We hurried through the light rain to Nic's apartment on the second floor, and we ignored our packages in favor of other pleasures entirely.

The first thing she did was undress me, letting my pink trench coat and pale peach sundress fall to the floor before sliding my slim white hipsters down past my ankles and waiting for me to step out of them. She didn't say a word about my tie-up espadrilles—a bad choice for a rainy day, but a good choice for stand-up sex—and I guessed that she liked the way I looked in them. I felt like a movie star, glamorous and wanted.

The second thing she did was say, "Now, show me."

"Show you?" I echoed.

"With someone new, I need to learn."

"Show you what?"

"Touch yourself. Show me what you like."

And all at once, I was back in my old self. A person who could have been the inspiration behind the cliché *she doesn't know her ass from her elbow.* I felt naked—which, of course, I was—but not in a good way. I felt as if she'd found me out, and that I'd be destined to be one of those people who circles blocks endlessly with a right-turn signal indicator on, always gazing out the window to find the address.

"Come on, Cat," she insisted. "Show me."

"I've never, really—" I stammered.

"I want to know what's going on with you down there—"

Down there. God, she'd said those two words. Those scary two words. Said them as if she understood that "down there" to me was that distant region I'd never mastered. The wilds. The wilderness. The unexplored territory. Down there translated in my mind as the equivalent of "the new land" to my European ancestors of five hundred years ago.

"Come on," she said. "Don't be so shy. I've seen you, Cat. I know what you've got in you—"

"But really—" I started, and then I stopped. "What do you mean?"

"You're always where I am. It's as if you and I were destined to be on this same track. You're ready to let go. I can tell. So let go for me—"

And I thought about my vision: me in the ring, gazing out at the crowd. And I thought about Tracey, unable to ask for directions. And I said, "Please. I want to. But you help me—"

She took my fingers and wet them with her own mouth. Then

she knelt on the floor in front of me and parted my pussy lips herself. "Touch," she said. "Here."

I waited for a moment, hoping inspiration would strike. In a way, it did. Or really, she did. Like a guide, she showed me what to do. I let her work my fingertips over my clit—my clit! *There* it was after all this time!—and then she used two fingers of her own to slip inside me, curling them toward the front of my body—and Jesus, was that my G-spot?! How had she found it so quickly, and why were my knees threatening to give out?

I pushed back, so that I could lean on the wall behind me, and I spread my legs wider apart. The pleasure pulsing through me gave me the confidence to probe deeper. I used one hand to hold my lips open myself, and the other to tap gently against my clit. Oh, yes, that did feel good. Why hadn't I done something like that before? I didn't know I'd like it, but now I did. I gave myself little pats with my four fingers together. Then I used just two fingers, my middle and my pointer, and I rubbed over my clit again and again. The wetness spilled out of me, and I used my own rich gloss to keep my fingertips running smoothly, pushing me higher and harder and further.

Nicole stayed with me, fucking me with her overlapping fingers, but paying very careful attention to the way I worked myself. It was as if she were trying to learn from me—from me!—and I thought once again of how Tracey had always acted in her irritating know-it-all manner in bed, sure that she could get me off, and determined to make me feel as if it were my fault when she failed.

But I wasn't going to fail this time. I was Christopher Columbus, and there was land right in my sight. Treasure awaited me. The reward was so close I could see the glittering gold, the shimmering gems. My fingers moved faster and faster. Why had they never known to do this in the past? I don't know. Perhaps, this experience was like those stories of people who travel with one partner and have a miserable trip, and then return to a site with someone new and reconstruct a whole new experience....

Now, I was going to come.

Oh, *yes*. I was going to come. And Nicole, so easygoing, so vigilant, was going to watch.

"Hold on," she said, removing her hand quickly, then standing and picking me up in her strong arms. She carried me to the bedroom and spread me out, then took up her watching position again, her face close to my pussy, so close that she could flick her tongue out and touch me in between strokes of my fingertips.

"Please—" I groaned, arching my hips.

"No," she said, "you do it. I'm just helping."

So I did. I worked for it, striving to set my foot on that distant soil. I thought of exotic locations, faraway regions where pretty girls place a lei over your neck when you step off the plane, and I thought of the paradise right here in Nicole's bedroom. My fingertips crested along my clit, and I knew the second before I came that it was going to happen. After years of no success, I was going to come.

Nicole knew, too. At the very last moment, she moved my hand aside and locked her lips around my clit, sucking in a rhythm that matched the touch my fingers had employed, rocking me with the force of her mouth and her hands gripped into my hips.

God, was that good. She knew so much about "down there," as if she'd been before. As if she visited often. Every weekend, and vacations, too.

And in fact, she does now. She spends all her free time down there. Learning. Memorizing. Teaching me something new. Because isn't that what good travel is all about? Exploring the unknown while opening up new horizons in ourselves?

TO THE POINT

Rita Winchester

want you to put them in tonight," I breathe. I say it softly because I'm a little embarrassed but loud enough that David can hear me over the radio. The small red car barrels down the dark beach road and I hold my breath. I also hold on tightly to the handle above my door.

His face is lit with a haunting green light from the dashboard. He turns to look at me, dirty blond hair hanging over his bright green eyes. In this light, with that look, he can morph in an instant. One glance shows me a little boy regarding me. Then I blink, and a dangerous man with an almost cruel smile is staring back. "I don't know."

"Please." I hate how needy I sound but it turns me on, too. The urgent nature of my voice makes me push my volume just a bit higher. "Please," I repeat because his only answer has been to smile.

He takes one hand from the steering wheel and puts it in my lap. He pushes his long fingers up under the open leg of my shorts and worms past my panties. He finds me wet and ready and pushes his fingers into me so hard I gasp. But I also slide down to let him in deeper. "You really do. You're wet for it, aren't you, Betsy?"

His laugh makes my skin pebble with a combination of fear and excitement. I nod and watch the twin points of gold from the headlights drill into the black, black night.

"We'll see," he says, and I let myself inhale. "We'll see" usually means "yes." After all, everyone wins in this scenario. But sometimes David denies me what I ask for just so I will remember that he can. That he is the one in charge. But he loves to hear me beg, so I have my own cards to play in this game.

"Thank you."

He parks in front of the small beach house and I inhale the warm night air. It smells of salt and pine and far-off board-walk smells. His aunt has let us stay for the weekend, other-wise, we would never be able to afford such a quaint cottage so close to the beach. Out here there are no streetlights, no city noises, no nothing. It is pitch-black, with nothing around us but the old pines that surround the house tower. We are so very secluded and yet I feel so vulnerable, as if I am on display. Fear makes my skin tingle and then my cunt grow wet. It is the fear of the deadly I abhor and I crave. I sigh without realizing it. When David frowns, I hear my own sound as if on delay.

"Don't pout, Betsy, or the answer will be no."

My body grows warmer. That means the answer is yes. When he holds out his hand, I take it. He sits me on the glider on the big wooden porch. I feel like every feral thing that may be in the woods can see me. Anything could swoop out of the night and eat me up. Rip me to shreds. I am a victim.

David plucks my nipple hard and laughs. "You're such a fear

slut. I bet if I pinched you a few more times, you'd come all over your lovely black panties."

I hum deep in my throat and try not to respond. If I am not afraid enough, he will be angry. If I am too afraid, he will be annoyed. Silence or just sounds are my best bet. His fingers test me again and my cunt contracts around his probing digits. I'm so eager I feel dizzy.

"Don't move. I'll be right back."

I sit. I listen to the night sounds: owls and crickets, something shifting in the underbrush, something else skulking in the crawl space under the house. It is right below my feet and the terror that I feel rears up black and horrible and wonderful, too. My legs go numb and I doubt I could run if I wanted to. The adrenaline and anxiety have hobbled me. I know it is only a raccoon or a possum, some innocent creature, but in my mind it is something sinister with claws and glowing eyes and blood lust.

I want to cry out for David but I don't. If I cry out for help I will be punished. For one thing, he will leave me out here all night. For another, he will not wear them for me. He won't let me get off and get it out of my system, for another day or week or month if I'm lucky.

The time drags out, and I can feel my own wet excitement between my legs. I can feel the places where I have leaked a bit drying on my skin. There it will mingle with the salty mist that has left a dry sheen on my tanned skin. I listen as hard as I can to hear David inside, and I hear nothing more than frightening sounds from the woods around me. My pulse is beating hard in my throat and tears have begun to form in my eyes.

Something moves down below the porch rail to my left. My heart seizes up and I clench my hands into fists. There is something very real out there and I don't know what it is. I go to cross my legs and stop. If David finds me that way, he will deny me for at least a week and a week is unthinkable. I force myself to stay as still as a statue. If it is a bear I will die. The thought of a bear and then of death is enough to clench my stomach into a tight knot. More tears and I sniffle as softly as I can.

"Betsy," comes the singsong voice. It is full of dark cruelty. My pussy pulses and my nipples peak harder. They hurt, they are so hard, and my soft cotton tank is an almost unbearable burden. "You've been a bad, bad girl. Kinky girl. Filthy little slutty girl," he rasps.

It is my David in a long dark coat. His hair is combed back, and with it all pushed back the pale planes of his face are animalistic. When he smiles, the small amount of light from the full moon reflects knife edges of light off his teeth. His canines, wickedly sharp and made just for him. For me. I whimper but don't speak.

He moves forward, up the steps, and his natural grace shines through. That is why he has meshed with my lifelong fantasy perfectly. He has the grace and the air and the arrogance of my fantasy. When I confessed my needs, he purchased the props and we lived it out. I win. He wins. We all win in the vampire game.

I know those teeth will be on me, and I can hardly sit still. His lips and his tongue will work me over but it will be the teeth that make me come. He reaches down and hooks his big hand in the waistband of my shorts and tugs me to my feet. I am buzzing with adrenaline and I can barely move.

"Out of these, Betsy," his voice skates over my skin like a third hand. He pushes at my shorts and panties, tugs at my top. Then I am bare in the warm air and cool moonlight, naked and vulnerable to this predator.

David sinks to his knees and the black jacket rustles around him. He begins the slow dangerous drag of his teeth up my inner thigh. I throw my head back, lost in it. His tongue flicks in and out and wets my skin, but it is the sensation of those dangerous canines on my skin that makes my cunt contract and spasm. He slides a finger into me and laughs against my skin. I am so wet, he could slide all of his fingers in without effort.

He bites me at the crux of my thigh. There will be marks but not blood. One day, I will ask him to puncture me, but for now the purple and pink tattoos of our sessions are enough. The marks of him eating me up that will last for days are a beautiful thing.

"Spread your legs wider, little girl." He doesn't wait, but forces my stance wide. I fight to keep my balance.

I push my hips forward, begging him to make me come and praying he will not. Not yet. I need more. David gives it to me. He moves to the other side and puts a daisy chain of bite marks up my inner thigh until I am thrusting my hips without thought, until that lone finger in my cunt has me half insane.

When he latches on to my clit with his lips only, bright white sparks rain down like shooting stars beneath my eyelids. He suckles with his innocent soft lips until I am right on the edge. Then he backs off to torture me with a well-placed bite to the fleshy part of my hip. I moan and shift, forcing my mound against his chin.

"Whore," he laughs but returns, this time with his tongue. Up and down he swoops with his gorgeous wet tongue. I hold my breath as he licks me with a broad flat stroke. My cunt coils, I am so close. He can smell it on me, taste it and feel it, because he rears back again and bites me right above my pelvic bone, mere inches below my belly button. The skin there is fragile and soft and he bites me hard.

The first warm spasm uncurls in me. "Oh." That's all I can say.

David adds two more fingers to my weeping pussy and then it

is the teeth he puts to me. He clamps on to the swollen battered nub of my clitoris and bites. Bites me until white noise roars in my ears and I come, sobbing from the pain and the pleasure of it all.

David stays on his knees lapping at me with his tongue, soothing the pain he has inflicted. I give him one more slow languid orgasm before dropping to my knees. I find him in the folds of black fabric, run my hand up the hard ridge of his cock, find his zipper, and set him free.

He growls at me and the fear returns, hot and white in the dark silent night. "I need you, sir," I say to my captor. My undead visitor. My lover. Now I have to suck him. I will suck him and he will fuck me. Long and slow. And at the very end, he will bite me again. I say it all out loud with a brave kind of dread. Because when it comes to this—what I need—I have to be to the point.

HOLD ON, I'M COMING

Kristina Wright

Motown gets me hot. Something about those old songs—the rhythm and soul and passion—gets me wet. I'll be cleaning house with the stereo tuned to the oldies station and one minute I'm tossing a load of whites into the laundry and the next minute I'm getting myself off to Marvin Gaye singing "Let's Get It On," hand in my pants stroking my clit in time to the music. Maybe it's the lyrics to those old songs that get me going. Whatever it is, I can't resist it. I need to get it on—immediately!

Those songs are so filled with innuendo and raw sensuality that I can imagine being fucked nine ways to Sunday to an all-Motown soundtrack with a different position for every song. In fact, it's kind of a long-standing fantasy of mine to do just that. I start gyrating to the music as if I were a pole dancer and I can't keep my hands out of my panties. I've had more orgasms to Motown than I can count, and every time a new "Best of" CD comes out, I buy it—looking for new old songs I haven't come to yet. Motown as stroke material has always been my little secret. Until recently, that is.

I was scrubbing down the shower stall in the bathroom one Sunday—my husband Eric off on a bunch of errands that would take him to both a home improvement store and an electronics store—knowing I had hours of alone time. When "Baby I Need Your Loving" started playing, my hips started swaying and my mind started drifting to hot, sexy images. By the time the Four Tops had faded and the Isley Brothers were wailing about "This Old Heart of Mine," I was sprawled across our unmade bed, naked except for my panties. I slid my hand under the waistband, gasping at how wet I already was. My nipples pebbled up hard and aching and I pinched them lightly, feeling a corresponding zing between my thighs. I rocked my hips up for an imaginary lover whose heart had been broken a thousand times, wanting to please him and come for him.

That's the way Eric found me.

I was sliding two fingers deep inside my wet pussy when I heard a sound and opened my eyes. Eric stood at the end of the bed, grinning like a madman. Though I'm well past the age of consent and it was my own bed and I was alone, I jerked upright, blushing and stammering.

"I thought you were going to be gone awhile."

He cocked an eyebrow at my crotch, my hand still in my panties and my fingers still buried in my pussy. "Clearly."

"Uh, yeah, well…"

Almost reluctantly, I took my hand out of my panties, my fingers glistening. I was a little irritated by his intrusion on my private time; irritated and still horny as hell. What could I say, though? I'd been caught red-handed.

"Want some help with that?" he asked as Mary Wells started singing "My Guy." I love that song.

"Yeah?"

"Take off the panties," he said by way of a response.

Hot and needy, I shimmied out of my panties before Mary got to the part about her guy being "cream of the crop."

Still fully clothed, Eric got on the bed. "Lie down."

I stretched out and Eric nestled between my spread legs, propping himself on his elbows. He looked up at me from between my thighs. "What do you want, baby?"

"I *need* to get off," I murmured, running my hand through his hair and giving it a tug toward my crotch. "Lick me."

My pussy ached to be touched, but Eric just blew cool air across my engorged clit. I rocked my hips up in response to the tingling sensation, whimpering in my need for more. He teased me, withholding what I needed so badly as "Ain't Too Proud to Beg" started. I didn't care what the Temptations said, I was *not* going to beg for what I needed.

I closed my eyes and focused on the music, determined to wait him out. I wasn't *that* desperate to come. He blew on my clit again and I could feel my juices trickling down my pussy. There would be a wet spot on the bed before we were done. I arched up toward his mouth again, but he evaded me. I moaned and he chuckled.

"I need to come," I said, giving in. Begging. "Please make me come."

He touched the tip of his tongue to my quivering clit, and I thought I was going to go through the roof. It felt so good—warm and velvety against my aroused clit—and I whimpered for more. He licked me then, the broad flat of his tongue stroking my entire pussy and coming to rest on my clit. Again and again his tongue ran up between the lips of my pussy to the rhythm of the old classics. He lapped me slowly to Jimmy Ruffin's melancholy "What Becomes of the Brokenhearted" and faster to "It's the Same Old Song." I'd masturbated a hundred times to the Four Tops singing that song, and it really did have a different meaning when it was Eric getting me off instead of my own fingers.

Over the music, I could hear him licking me, and the sound of his tongue in my wetness was erotic and tender. He stroked my sensitive flesh slowly and sensually, as if he had all the time in the world to pleasure me like this. I had no objections to that idea, but I needed to come. Ached for it. Now. I clutched at his hair, rocking my hips against his warm mouth, moaning as he gave me everything I needed. By the time The Temptations started crooning "The Way You Do The Things You Do," I knew Eric was going to send me over the razor-sharp edge of desire and into an orgasm so intense I would never again be able to get off to Motown without thinking of his tongue devouring my cunt like an overripe piece of fruit.

"Oh, god, lick me," I demanded, my voice sounding almost like a growl. "Right there, yeah. Oh, baby, I need to come so bad."

The Miracles started singing "You Really Got a Hold on Me" as Eric took my swollen, sensitive clit between his lips. He sucked it gently and every nerve ending in my body throbbed, trembling with a need so great it was more than physical. Hot tears trickled from the corners of my eyes, my mind and body so overwhelmed by sensation I couldn't contain it any longer. I clamped my damp thighs around his head, rocking to his rhythmic sucking and licking as he gave me my own little personal miracle and I started to come.

Every muscle in my body contracted then and I doubled over the top of his head, smelling my arousal hanging heavy in the air. I clutched at his shoulders, my legs wrapped around his back as his tongue milked every ounce of sensation from my swollen clit.

"Put your fingers in me," I gasped.

He quickly slipped two fingers deep inside me, and I whimpered as my pussy contracted around him. My swollen G-spot gushed, making the wet spot beneath me even bigger as he finger-fucked me and sucked my clit. I bucked against him like a wild thing, moaning and gasping for breath but unwilling to tell him to stop because it just felt so damned good. I came until my stomach muscles ached and the insides of my thighs felt raw from his beard stubble.

Finally, slowly, he stopped licking my oversensitive clit and withdrew his fingers from my dripping pussy. I lay back on the bed, glistening with sweat and gasping for breath. It was then that I realized I didn't even know what song had been playing when I started coming. Tammi Terrell was singing "You're All I Need to Get By" to Marvin Gaye now, and I started giggling uncontrollably. Eric slid up the bed beside me, stroking my trembling stomach and looking at me with puzzlement.

"Not quite the reaction I was going for," he said.

I shook my head. "Just listen."

Aretha sang what I was feeling about what he'd done to me. I was exhausted, satisfied, and very, very happy he had come home early. I was still quivering in the aftermath of my orgasm, but my imagination was racing toward all those songs I loved and all those sexual positions I wanted to try. I curled around Eric, no doubt leaving a wet spot on his jeans.

"Want some for yourself?" I purred.

He put my hand on his sizeable bulge. "What do you think?"

I giggled again as I unfastened his belt, my desire satiated, but still humming beneath the surface of my sweat-slick skin.

"Just one thing," he said, as I worked his zipper down.

"What?"

"Can we change the station? I hate this old stuff."

DROPPING THE HINT

Drew James Dyer

My wife has one or two eccentric habits.

I should explain, first, that Dora keeps early hours at the chemistry lab, where she and two other graduate students arrive at six a.m. daily; eat lunch at ten; and lock up at three. Personally, I don't see why the inorganic molecules that Dora studies should force her out of bed at five a.m.—that would seem more fitting in a field like botany or zoology, where everyone's up with the sun. But my understanding of chemistry, like my understanding of most things outside the world of finance, is limited, and perhaps the experts have determined that nitrogen and helium are at their friskiest at breakfast time.

And so Dora gets home before me, five days a week, and has ample opportunity to shed her work clothes, shower, and slip into the special lab coat that she uses as a dressing gown. It's a sort of minidress-length garment in an absurdly bright shade of white, which boasts scientifically credible long sleeves and yet forces her panties to peek out beneath the hem. I have no idea where she obtained it (campus supply or fetish boutique?), but she says it's very comfortable.

I come through the door a few hours later, an impeccable accountant who is hopelessly disorganized and indecisive outside his office. I rumble in precariously like a badly packed luggage cart, ready as I'll ever be to enter the slightly baffling world of private life after another proud day of fiscal magic.

Each time I cross the threshold, I feel a wave of gratitude for the fact that Dora runs our life. My guiding principle is that if a matter can't be settled by recourse to a printing calculator, then I don't want to be the one in charge.

Dora, as I said, has one or two eccentric habits, and she often greets me at the door with a laboratory-grade eyedropper behind her back.

You see, she likes to drop me hints, in liquid form. So she's taught me a variety of signals, instructing me in the semaphore that she operates via small samples of fluid. When she smiles and says "Tongue"—where many a spouse might say "Hello"—I close my eyes and render the aforementioned organ accessible to her. I must look quite a spectacle, sticking my tongue out like a brat in a custom-tailored suit, but it's for Dora.

Sometimes I taste a drop of olive oil, meaning that it's my turn to cook. A flash of red wine from the eyedropper, and I know we're dining out. Worcestershire sauce indicates that my mother has phoned and is expecting me to call back. Lemonade translates into movie night.

But tonight is even more special than movie night. I know this because after I walk in the door—and am duly prompted to extend my tongue—I taste a drop of something that doesn't come out of any bottle in our well-appointed kitchen.

I taste a drop of Dora, of Dora's pussy juice. In a glorious moment of sensation, I experience that complex collaboration of something that tastes a little bit like lime and something that tastes a little bit like mulled wine…and an assortment of other feminine elements that taste like—well, like I'm about to cream myself.

The sample is fresh as hell, and I know that while she listened to my car in the driveway, she was bending over, flipping her lab coat hem up with her left hand, and using her right hand both to edge her knickers out of the way and to suck her fluid into the dropper. She doesn't need to be in that position to get the sample, of course, but she showed me once how she does it, and it's just as I've described. Dora is dramatic, even when she's alone in the house. Moreover, the position itself makes her wet. She explained this to me that first time, as she pumped the little black bulb and gave up her essence in a beautiful travesty of science.

You may have surmised, more or less, what a drop of Dora on my tongue signifies in our house. That it doesn't have anything to do with calling my mother, for instance.

And tonight, I don't get merely the one drop. Just when I'm about to open my eyes, I feel a second drop, then a third, and each tastes more essential than the previous one. The flavor of Dora's femininity awakens taste buds I'm otherwise unaware of possessing. More and more of my tongue tingles with each drop. It's now a long enough series of drops that I've lost count, despite my proficiency with numbers, and my mouth—my entire head— is so full of her that it's almost too much delight to contain. I feel an impossible, animal impulse for an instant, like I want to shove my cock into my own mouth and fuck the hell out of my nectar-infused tongue. But as her juice soaks into me, I calm down just enough to proceed rationally. I finally open my eyes.

She smiles, then leaves me standing there with her taste in my mouth.

I still have my briefcase in my hand, and as I hold it idly at waist level I feel my cock pressing against it, tingling through my trousers against the attaché's resistance.

The briefcase gets put where it belongs—the stool by the microwave—but my cock will need to bide its time. Because those drops of Dora in my mouth lead my mouth straight back to Dora. Meaning that other parts of my anatomy just have to get in line.

She's still in her lab coat when I reach the bedroom, but her pink panties are gone. She's facedown and squirming a bit. I know that on drop-of-Dora nights, she's already worked up by the time I get home, and she can barely stand to wait. In fact, I think she sometimes sneaks in a quick warm-up round without me.

Yes, Dora runs our life, and I'm never disappointed in the results. She has everything figured out, and when she serves up her cunt, I know it's because my mouth upon her wetness is what she wants more than anything in the world—more than food, more than sleep, and a lot more than a movie.

Her ass looks birthday-cake sweet beneath the kinky laboratory housecoat. I see it for just a moment until, sensing my presence, she rolls onto her back and spreads her legs.

I'm still dressed in a suit, and I'm practically hobbling due to my hard-on. I quickly undress, and when I sit down on the bed, at Dora's feet, I see that she's still clutching the eyedropper. It was in her right hand before; now it's in her left, which makes me think that she was using her dominant hand, during the moments she awaited me here, for something more skill specific, something between her thighs.

She sits up, and she hands me the dropper. Her legs remain generously apart, and it's easy for me to procure what's needed. I bring the dropper, now full, to her mouth, and she drinks of herself greedily while I finger the bulb for her. Then she takes the dropper from my hand and sets it aside. She reclines again, and her legs swing open even farther. She is closer to one side of the bed than the other, and her left ankle dangles over the edge.

As I lift what little bit of her garment is obstructing complete, devoted access to her pussy, I am overwhelmed by the beauty of this: the beauty of believing that I have no doubt what Dora desires. She has communicated it to me, after all, in a socially idiosyncratic but chemically accurate manner. I don't even have to think, to worry for a second about whether I'm giving her what she needs.

I grasp her thighs and plunge my face into her female folds. I can still feel the blessing of the eyedropper, nurturing me like a nipple, guiding me unambiguously with Dora's flavor. And as I deliver the first genital kiss I am staunchly confident, as is the stiff cock that I'm carrying like unchecked baggage.

Her cunt lips quiver a mixture of luscious relief and heightened tension, as the contact with my mouth both gratifies and escalates her need. I make a full tour of her pussy's perimeter with my kisses, knowing that she wants to feel my warm, heavy lips at all points on the edge of her passion before my tongue works its shrinking circles toward her center. I visit her beautifully engorged clit, and the nub reminds me of the eyedropper bulb. I suck it softly, and the increased flow of liquor from Dora's gap plays to my concept that I'm bringing forth her wetness by squeezing her little bulb. Then I release it so that I can take another lap around the course.

My cock pulses crazily as her liquid accosts my chin with a desperate lewdness. I take the briefest instant to savor the sight of her wet vulva, to glow with the incomparable buzz of knowing—of seeing, smelling, and tasting—that Dora wants me, that Dora needs me, that every bit of Dora's pussy is writhing in moisture-saturated anticipation of the moment that my tongue will lick her fully. It makes me feel like I actually know what I'm doing.

As I start to lick into her, I note that the taste of Dora on Dora is even fresher than what the eyedropper had bestowed on me. When my tongue tastes her fluid straight from the walls of her cunt, it's as if I'm drinking it right from the innermost depths of her sexual self—like I have a direct line to the churning reservoir of lust that bubbles beneath the outer Dora day after day, until the day it seeps to the surface and suffuses us both with the potent chemistry of desire. The day—such as today—that she greets me with it at the door, her arousal on tap and samples on the house.

I lick inward and around, with enough pressure that I'm soaking up her juice like a paper towel. But there is, miraculously, an endless supply of juice. Fortunately, my tongue is infinitely absorbent—a claim not shared by even the most aggressively marketed paper towel. And, unlike the typical kitchen spill-jockey, I am not eager to mop up and move on. On the contrary, I feel like I could lick Dora's cunt, in luxurious slow motion, all night long.

But this is no infinite plateau; it's not what a chemist would call a "steady state." Slowly but surely, her moaned responses evolve from passionate to urgent. Her body's demands implore me from all sides—the puffed pussy lips that need my kisses, harder kisses this time; the clit that sizzles for the precise flick of an accountant's tongue tip; the seething cunt walls, which bathe themselves in a liquid graffiti that begs me to return soon.

I do my best to accommodate all of this. Insofar as it is possible, my lips are everywhere and my tongue is a blur of motion, like an electron in orbit. And this is how it should be, for Dora is my nucleus and, at the moment, Dora's pussy is the nucleus of the nucleus, the all-important center of my immediate

universe; the delicious core of the world, giving me sweet suste-
nance, so generously that my face has become sticky with her
essence of life. "I love you! I love you!" Dora screams, a woman
who didn't even say hello at the door... "I love you," she wails,
as her delicate flesh spasms and weeps. Pussy juice pools where
the hem of her lab coat touches the bed, and her clit seems to
embody yet another heartfelt *I love you* as it strains against
my tongue.

My cock is rigid to the point of near-paralysis, and yet I'd
almost forgotten about it. But Dora hasn't forgotten. And as she
puts me where I need to be now, I feel her washing me with wet
shudders. At below-the-waist level, I wallow inside her, twitching
and building to paradise; but my consciousness is really in my
mouth, which now rests against the base of her neck. I relish
the lingering flavor of her sauce, hoarding her inside me even
as I nibble gently at the skin of her shoulder and my hips buck
uncontrollably down below. Our groins seem as far away as
another county, though the echo of my orgasm, when it arrives,
rattles distinctly in my head.

At the office the next day, I find the eyedropper in the pocket
of my jacket. I'm sure I didn't put it there—I'm disorganized,
but I'm not absentminded. I don't have to bring it to my face to
know that it hasn't been washed or even rinsed. Its irresistible
tang tickles my nostrils as I cradle it in the palm of my hand.

I can't concentrate on forms and figures, and I spend hours
wondering what Dora will want me to do when I get home. She's
never left me in charge of the dropper for more than a minute,
and my stomach flutters as if I've been awarded an exciting
but slightly intimidating promotion. But she obviously thinks
I can handle it, and this reassures me. I remember the luxury
in her smile yesterday, right after I'd tongued and tasted her
into ecstasy.

I'm hard again, and a drop of precome crowns my throbbing nostalgia for drop-of-Dora night. I am a happy man at a desk, sucking on a dry eyedropper while the building empties around me into lunchtime bliss.

PAUSE

Sommer Marsden

Y ou okay?"

I sniffled and wiped my eyes hurriedly. I hadn't seen Tom coming as I headed out for a much-needed walk. The bright sunlight had blinded me to his presence. I had turned and he was there.

"Fine. I'm fine," I lied. "The wind."

"Right. The wind. How about a nice hot cup of very expensive coffee to curb the wind's effects? It's cold as hell."

He rattled a Zeke's bag at me. I knew what that meant. Inside would be half a pound of the darkest, most decadent brew Zeke's Coffee made. I needed decadent because my life seemed to be drowning in darkness.

"Sure. Perfect. Just let me run home and get Jack." I lived four doors down from Tom.

"Jack is fine. He's a dog. He'll be just fine as he is. You are not. No matter what you say. Come on then." His crisp accent did odd things to me. When he told me secrets, it was like listening to a dirty bedtime story—the way his voice snaked into my ears and heated my blood.

I followed him up the three steps and into his small house. "You and Gordon?" He studied my face, puffy from crying, and nodded. I never said a word but he had his answer. "Sit." Tom busied himself with the coffee. I watched his lean, muscular back, the way his shoulders bunched and rippled when he reached for the filters; the play of the muscles in his lower back when he bent to find his grinder. I watched the easy way he moved and how very right he seemed, a man who was comfortable in his life, his body, his ways. I liked that. It made me feel stable. Gordon was a live wire: untamed, unhappy, a ball of kinetic energy that sucked the life from me most of the time.

My throat squeezed. My heart pounded. Tears came back to the surface just as Tom turned.

"Oh, love," he sighed and started toward me as my head fell forward. I tried to swallow a sob and half managed. What came out was more of a sorrowful moan. Then he was on his knees and his arms were around me. "None of that. He isn't worth it. Really."

I knew that. And it wasn't so much Gordon. It was me. I never seemed to get it right when it came to men. Never. Mostly, it pissed me off. At this moment in time, though, it made me sad, an intense sadness that settled low in my belly.

He smelled like coffee, tobacco, and cotton. I took a deep breath and tried to calm myself. When he looked up and smiled, I didn't think. I pressed my lips to his and tasted cigarettes and coffee and a sweet undertone that could only be him. Heat warmed me. Internal heat. It started in my throat and coursed through my breast, over my belly, and between my legs. I wanted his hands there. Between my legs. His face. His cock.

"Noelle. You need to stop that. Now." His voice was gruff

and despite my best efforts, my gaze was drawn to his lap. To the lovely hard cock that strained against his faded jeans. I reached for him, and he grabbed my wrist, hard. He squeezed and I winced.

"Why? I'm not that bad," I said, my voice fluttery from all the crying.

"You're not even slightly bad. But I wouldn't want to be that man."

He was staring at my mouth, my bottom lip. I bit it. It was dirty fighting I knew, but I did it anyway. I would fight dirty if I had to, for just one night with a man who wanted me, wanted to fuck me without consuming me or breaking me down. Who was secure enough to simply want me and then take me.

"What man?" I asked and leaned into him. I got as close to him as his strong grip would allow, blew a light breath over his throat. I noticed a small nick from shaving. I noticed how the stubble had already overtaken his small morning victory. Dark hair sprouted from his tanned skin. I wanted to rub my face against it, feel it against the fragile skin on the inside of my thighs.

"The one who takes advantage." His green eyes narrowed. He was serious, very intent on not hurting me. Those eyes grew darker as I moved closer. He was trying very hard to hold himself back. For me. That made me want him all the more.

"Take advantage of me. Please." I opened my thighs and he slid his big body between my legs. But he didn't kiss me. He watched me instead.

"It's wrong. What if you and Gordon work things out? What then?"

I shook my head. "It won't happen. All we do is fight. I was crying because I had decided it was over. I had officially given up on men."

"Ah, see. I'm a man," he said and tried to pull back. I shut my thighs as tight as I could.

"I know. But not the average man. You're different. I want you."

"You just think you do," he said. His gaze was back on my mouth.

"No," I said honestly. "For a while now. But I didn't think…" I leaned in and kissed him again. He pulled back, but not before I had felt his lips soften. He wanted to kiss me back.

"What. You didn't think what?" His voice was husky. His hands on me were harsh. I felt my cunt grow slicker. God, now that I was saying it, it made the want that much worse.

"That you would want me."

He let out a bark of laughter and tossed his head back. I leaned in and bit him just below the jaw, and the laughter turned to a growl. Tom yanked my jacket off. Then my sweater. He tugged at my jeans. His breathing was harsh, and I kicked my legs wildly to disengage the denim. Finally, I sat splayed in his wooden kitchen chair with nothing between us other than what he had on.

"I want you. That's not an issue," he said. It looked as if he wanted to say more but he didn't. Instead he took my white cotton tank that I'd had under my sweater. He moved behind me and gently tied my wrists together, anchoring them to the chair. "Now spread your thighs for me, Noelle. I've waited way too long for this."

In his sunny kitchen that smelled of good strong coffee and aroused woman, he knelt between my legs. He smelled me first, simply put his head between my thighs and inhaled deeply. A small bit of moisture seeped out of me. I felt it trickle down my skin. I held my breath. I watched. His green eyes found mine and he smiled. Slowly he stuck out his tongue and touched the tip, just the tip, of my throbbing clit.

I jumped as if I'd been electrocuted. I tested my bonds and found them tight.

"Easy. Behave yourself."

I nodded. I tried to breathe as his tongue blazed a hot trail over my slit and up over my clit. I swallowed a moan. I would not beg. I promised myself that. I wanted Tom, that was true. I had wanted him for a very long time. But this easy, lazy way of his was driving me mad.

"Spread them wider, love. I want to see it all. All of you."

I spread my legs as wide as I could, my belly fluttering with excitement and impatience. First, his eyes examined me, then his finger. He spread me wide and touched each bit of me: my outer lips, my wet entrance, my tender clit. I tried not to thrash under his touch. When he followed his finger with his tongue, my thighs tried to clamp around his head, tried to trap him where I wanted him. He took his big strong hands and forced my thighs wide again. I let my head fall back and I gasped for air.

I was right there. A few more flicks of his hot tongue and I could fall over that edge into bliss.

He stopped.

I waited but nothing came. I could feel his warm breath on my wet pussy. His hands still pried me open, his fingers on the soft skin of my inner thigh. He stroked me patiently, right there, maintaining the arousal but not finishing me off.

I raised my head. "What? Second thoughts?" I panted.

I thought I might cry.

Tom made a tsking sound. "You should know better. I plan to spend the rest of the day showing you just how very much I want you. How much I *have* wanted you. For a long, long time."

"But?" I asked. My body was clenching, demanding that what was started be finished. By him. He moved his fingers toward me and my pussy clenched with anticipation. He stopped, his finger just shy of me. I was left with nothing but the mental image of his fingers probing my cunt.

"This is just a pause. Be patient. It's almost over."

I wiggled in the chair, felt the wood peel away from my asscheeks. I tugged at my tank that bound my wrists. Any moment I was going to scream.

"A pause? What for?"

He traced my nipple with his finger and I arched up into his hand, ground my teeth together. I would have clamped my legs together but he had me pinned wide.

"It makes it that much better," he said. Keeping his eyes on mine, he bent low and blew lightly on my clit, arched his tongue to taste me and touch me. For one second. Precisely.

He sat back on his heels while my body seemed to hum. I wouldn't have been surprised if I started throwing off sparks.

"Please," I panted.

A finger slid into me and my head lolled back again. My cunt clutched around it. My hips shot up to meet him.

"You're being a fairly good girl," he said and added a second finger.

"Please. Please, Tom."

He took his good sweet time. He lowered his handsome head so slowly. He rubbed his stubbled cheek along my skin from the inside of my knee to the crux of my thigh. Then his tongue traced me and I bowed up in the chair, one taut muscle. My nipples peaked and I felt a fresh slide of fluid between my legs.

Slowly he licked me. He sucked my clit into his mouth and worked me with his tongue, then with his lips, until I was nearly sobbing with the want of it, the need of him. He pushed his tongue deep into me and fucked me with the rigid tip. Then he sucked me until I yanked at my bonds fiercely.

Then he stopped.

"Oh, my god! No way!" I was crying. Tears rolled down my cheeks, my body one big nerve ending.

"Just a pause."

"I'll kill you," I said. More tears. I should have felt ridiculous. Instead, I felt frantic.

"Shh. Shorter this time. You'll live."

"I don't think so." And I didn't. I thought I might actually die from hanging on the edge of orgasm. It felt that way. My body was so tight inside that there was nowhere left to go. I could come or go slowly insane. Those were my options.

"Shh. It will be fine. I promise," Tom said. He lowered his head and kissed my belly, his dark hair the color of Zeke's coffee on my pale skin. He kissed me right above my blonde patch of pubic hair, inches from my clit. He kissed me long and slow and soft, right there.

I cried some more.

"Don't cry."

"I want it."

"I know."

He kissed the very top of my thigh. Scant inches to the left of my sex.

"I need it."

"I know."

"Please, baby," I begged.

"If you insist," he said and moved quickly. He sucked me in. One swift motion. He captured my clit between his wet wet lips and pulled me into the blazing fire of his mouth.

One suck.

I came. I came and I yanked against the cotton tee that held me. I sobbed and I jumped. I thrashed like I was dying. Because I was. He was killing me slowly with his tongue, the most beautiful death I could imagine.

He kept at me gently for a few moments, kissing a bit, tasting me more. My lungs refused to work for a while, and I simply watched his dark head in my lap. He laid it there, just waiting. I think he was listening to the twitches and echoes of orgasm as they worked through my cunt, through my body.

I was loose. I was lazy. I felt like sunshine.

"Coffee?" he asked.

"Please. I can smell it. The smell is driving me crazy. The more I smell it. The more I want it."

He kissed my clit and I jumped a little. He stood, untied my wrists and said, "Sometimes the things we're forced to wait for are the very best things."

Then he kissed the back of my neck and I sighed.

ALL ABOUT THE GIRLS

Shanna Germain

In the winter, I sleep with boys. I love the way they look in turtleneck sweaters and jeans, their caps pulled down over their ears, the way their hair sprouts from unexpected alcoves of cheek and thigh. I love their heat, the way their bodies radiate warmth like living, breathing furnaces. In the winter, I like the way boys fill me, the hard coal of their bodies, the sweating, heavy heaters of their cocks inside me.

But in the summer, when the sun shimmies close in the sky and the AC is kicking, then, I'm all about the girls. The sparkling toes peeking out from sandals, the bits of skin between waistband and belly, between ankle and knee, hair swept up to show off the curve of the neck, the tiny *c* of an earlobe. The way girls walk, like me, slick and cool even in the heat, knowing that everyone is watching the backs of their calves against their skirts, the sway of their asses, those pinpoints of sweat at the bottoms of their spines.

There's one right now, sitting just in front of me at the coffee shop, pretending to read the paper. She's had the funnies section open now for twenty minutes, but I don't think she's interested in what Dagwood's got going on. Instead, she drums the side of her iced mocha with her French-tipped fingernails. She's wearing her sunglasses, trying to hide her eyes, but I know she's doing just what I'd be doing if I wasn't watching her—she's eying the girls who walk by outside the window.

Me, I'm watching her. From this angle, she's all legs in her short blue skirt and three-inch black sandals. Outside, a blonde girl in a perfectly cut A-line dress swings by, and this woman, she crosses and uncrosses those legs at the dimpled knees. I know she's trying to let a little air in there, to cool that hot spot between her thighs.

Even so, it's not her legs that draw me in. And it's not the tiny bit of pale bare skin showing between the skirt and her yellow T-shirt. It's not even the nipple bar that brackets her left nipple through the fabric, although I have to admit that's part of the appeal.

What's really getting to me are the tiny dark hairs escaping from the back of her sleek, shiny bun. Even in the coffee shop's struggling AC, those tiny hairs are sneaking out, falling into warm, wet curls against her skin. I take a sip of my coffee and watch the strands of her hair droop lazily, swing back up, tighten into curlicues.

She knows I'm watching—she ducks her head down to the comics and runs her index finger up and down her spine just below her hairline. Pinching a curl between her fingers, she pulls it down and out, straightens the damp hair. It's so blatantly erotic, so much like the movement I make with my own dark, damp curls that I have to put my cup of coffee back down on the table, press my fingers against the warm ceramic to keep them still. My insides start running rivers, a cool pulsing flow from my belly down into my thighs.

With one curl wrapped around her fingers, she pulls downward, a little harder, just enough to make her head fall back a little. My nipples respond, pushing out toward her, craving the pull of those fingers against their hardening centers. The ceramic cup burns through my fingers, but I hardly notice.

After a moment, she drops the curls, taps one pale-tipped finger against the back of her neck. It could be a habit. It could be an absentminded gesture. It could be an invitation.

I take it as an invitation. When I stand up, I'm dripping into the fabric of my skirt. I don't dare look at the chair I've just left. Instead, I come up from behind her. I clamp my fingers into her damp swirls of hair. Her curls are cool despite the sweat, rough and calming as a cat's tongue. I can't tell if anyone's looking, if anyone in the shop is playing witness to this. And at this moment, I don't really care.

She doesn't seem to care either. At least, she doesn't move away. Instead, she takes a long, slow sip of her iced mocha. The movement presses her head harder against my fingers, gives me more length of curl to wrap inside my hand. Still without moving away, she pushes the chair next to her away from the table with one long, sandal-finished leg. "Have you read your horoscope today?" she asks.

I shake my head no, and let my fingers drop from her curls. The inside of my palm is wet with sweat, hers and mine. When I sit next to her, the air around her swells with lavender and lemons. From here, I can see that both nipples are pierced—bars with balls that highlight her arousal. I imagine their steely coolness beneath my tongue, the way they will contrast to her hot skin.

She puts her finger to the Gemini sign and starts to read. I'm about to tell her that I'm a Cancer, not a Gemini, when she says, "The heat of the day could cause you to make unexpected decisions. Don't worry—by nightfall, it will all come clear. Between now and October, others will find you irresistible. Your lucky number is two."

She sets the paper on the table, open to the horoscope and crossword puzzle, and smoothes it down with her palms. "Sounds promising," she says. When she looks up at me, a few little curls have started beside her ears. I want to take them into my mouth and wet them into soft, sweet points. I can't look away from those curls, the way her eyes look intensely blue even through the light lenses of her sunglasses. I want to suck her coolness like a Popsicle.

While I'm still looking at her eyes, the iced mocha is suddenly against the outside of my leg, cool dripping cup pressed to the hot skin of my thigh. Normally, it's cold enough to make me jump, but now it just feels right, it feels good. It doesn't cool the heat that's between my thighs, though, and I don't want it to. I press my leg against her cup, opening my thighs just a little. "Good girl," she says. Her voice is so low I'm almost not sure I hear it beneath the music, the whirr of the coffee grinder, the voices of the couple at the next table. But then she says it again, "Good girl," and I get that river in my belly again, the current of cold that flows between my thighs.

Her leg is against the other side of the mocha, pressing the cold cup between our thighs. I catch a whiff of her: musk and chocolate—she's not wearing anything under that skirt. Anyone with enough balls and know-how could squat down right outside this coffee shop window and get one of the city's most amazing views. Instead, they're all walking on by, oblivious. I imagine her curls under there, just like the ones on her head, springing up tight from the heat and moisture. Just the thought of them, coarse and wiry, makes me put one hand back up to her neck, makes me pretend to brush something from her shoulder so I can feel the kink of her curls again. I give a tug and she opens her mouth, those lip-glossed red lips spreading just a bit. There is a sound, a hiss, a sigh, and then she closes her eyes behind her sunglasses.

The cup sears my leg with cold. I pull it out from between us and set it on the table, brushing my elbow against one of the metal bars inside her nipple. She moans low, sits up straight, and spreads her legs until her cool thigh is touching mine. Our skirts are almost the same length, baring long strips of thighs that touch skin to skin. Her skin is smooth and cool like I knew it would be.

I want to put my hands inside her skirt, to feel those curls. But despite everything, I'm nervous about the people around us. I've gone as far as I can in public, stretched my comfort level as far as it will go. So I sit there, letting her thigh spread its chill into my core; still feeling the drag of her cold, hard piercing against the skin of my elbow.

Just as things have the potential to turn awkward, she drops her hand into the purse that's hanging on her chair. Pen in hand, she leans forward over the crossword puzzle. "I try to do this every day," she says. She tilts her head to the side a little, looks at me over the top of her sunglasses. The sun through the windows turns her already blue eyes to sky. "I'd love a little help," she says.

I nod, still watching her eyes. She's got naturally dark eyelashes out to there. More curls that I want lick. I imagine her eyelids will taste like salt and lemons. She puts cool fingers against my arm. With her other hand, she clicks the pen, writes something in the first set of boxes. "Does that look right?" she asks.

I lean forward and look at the clue: *Ringlet of hair.* I start to say *curl,* and then realize she's already filled in the boxes in square handwriting. *5422,* it says. I don't know what it means.

Her fingers are still against my arm. They're all I can feel, the cool tips chilling my skin. She slides her chair back away from the table with a quiet squeak. "I guess I'd better hit the restroom," she says. Her purse is over her shoulder. I watch her walk away. She is slick and cool in the heat, knowing that I'm watching the curve of her calves against the back of her skirt, the sway of her ass, the tiny curls beneath the back of her sleek bun.

She reaches up with one hand, pulls the curls at the back of her neck out straight, and then I realize: 5422. The restroom code. The fact that she knows the code makes me hesitate—does she do this all the time? Does she work here? Then I remember those curls, rough and cool, and I realize I don't care.

I force myself to wait as long as I can before I rise, trying to act casual. My fingers shake when I punch the code into the box. When I turn the handle, I'm sure it will be stuck, locked from the inside. But instead, it opens to her long form, leaning back against the far wall. Not even the toilet beside her, the nearly overflowing garbage can, can take away the length of those legs, the blue of those eyes. I let the door shut behind me, step my way closer to her.

The AC doesn't seem to reach in here—the air is slow and dull as thick coffee. Tiny drips of sweat form against my cheeks. The hair against the back of my neck is damp. I am close enough to smell her lemon skin when she reaches around the back of my head, wraps her fingers up in my wet hair. She pulls me close and her tongue enters my mouth, all coffee and chocolate. The bars in her nipples press through her shirt. I take one in my fingers, twist it just slightly to the side, feeling nipple and metal move together until she moans inside my mouth.

So fast I surprise myself, I drop my hand and reach under her skirt, slide it up the inside of her thigh. She spreads her legs a little, and my fingers land, finally, in her other curls. They are thick and moist, the perfect length. I clamp a couple of the curls between my fingers, pull them straight down. With the other hand, I push her skirt up toward her waist. She scoots forward, lets me slide the fabric up until she can hold it against the wall with her body.

The skirt makes a wide belt across her belly. Now she is all wet curls and legs. I drop down on my knees, welcoming the cool tiles against my skin, the hot of her center against my fingers. I work her curls without touching her—tugging and pulling on the hairs, opening her up. I dig my tongue through her curls, along the edge of the thin strip of warm wetness between them.

"Wait," she says. Without moving away from the wall, she opens her purse and pulls out a purple package. She rips it open and spreads a thin sheet of latex between her legs. "I'll hold it," she says, and she does, with one hand in front and one in back.

I'm a little disappointed—I'd wanted to taste her—but I'm grateful, too. And when I put my tongue against her, I can still feel her heat even through the dam. The latex tastes like vanilla, but beneath that, I can smell her own caramel and chocolate sweetness. She is already wet and loose, open enough that I can slide my tongue across the sweet warm caramel of her, run it from back to front. Her clit is easy to find—already pointed and nubby. I run over the point of it with the flat of my tongue and she slides down lower, presses herself against me.

"There," she says, more breath than word, and my clit tightens at the sound. The heat of her is on my tongue, my cheeks. With both hands, I grasp the curls that escape the dam and pull them outward until she opens for me even more beneath the latex.

I blow against the dam, feel the little bubble of air between her skin and the latex. I trap the air and her clit lightly between my teeth, rub it back and forth. Far above me, she exhales air like a fan that's just been turned on.

She bucks against my mouth, once, twice. I still her by wrapping my fingers tighter in her curls, and then I take her clit into my mouth and suck hard, harder. Her hips are out, out away from the wall, into my mouth. Her clit bangs against my tongue. Again, harder, until she's doing all the moving and I'm just holding my tongue against the point of her, feeling her slicken and tighten.

"Yes, there," she says again, but she doesn't know what she's saying. It's just something to say as she comes, as she shivers a little and pulls her clit and curls away from my tongue. She covers herself, the latex, with her hand, lets her head fall back against the wall with a *thunk*.

I'm still on the knees on the floor, my nipples and clit throbbing, when she sighs, long and slow. "Jesus," she says. "Nothing like a, uh, daily crossword to get you going." Then she strips the latex away from her skin carefully and tosses it into the garbage. She reaches a damp hand down to my own. "Celia," she says as she pulls me to my feet. "Hi."

I don't say anything. It takes all my energy to pretend I'm not having trouble standing. She pulls her skirt back down, gives it a quick tweak so the zipper's on the side where it belongs. She runs a finger up the back of her neck to where those curls are now sweat-stuck to her skin. So it *is* a habit, not an invitation. "Wait five minutes," she says.

I nod. I'm not sure I could walk yet if I had to. I watch her slip out the door, calf muscles tight, her ass swaying just a little in that skirt—and I realize I haven't said a damn thing to this woman. Not one damn word. And I realize I don't want to. I just want to follow her wherever she's willing to take me. After all, it's summer and in the summer, I'm all about the girls.

THE DOMINANCE OF THE TONGUE

Teresa Noelle Roberts

Serena rose from Garth and Alison's pool, looking, to Jack's sun- and lust-dazzled eyes, like a deity in a zebra-striped bikini.

How did she do it?

Before they'd headed to the pool party, he'd spanked her, spanked her until she was red-assed and wet and squirming and begging, then told her to bring herself off for him. She'd obeyed, her eyes glassy with lust and a huge smile on her face, shoving three fingers into herself and teasing her clit until she came, her eyes fixed the whole time on the erection he was stroking as he watched. As soon as she'd come, she'd been on her knees in front of him and he'd had his cock in her mouth, fucking it like a pussy, until he'd shot down her throat.

On the way over to Garth and Alison's, he'd informed her that she was to do anything he asked of her, sexually, that day. He hadn't been sure whether she'd go for it, whether she wanted to extend their games of dominance and submission that far, but she'd smiled and complied with a lustful quiver in her voice. He'd given her an out then, told her she could back out if something sounded completely unappealing, but there'd be consequences later—"fun ones, but still a little painful," he'd specified. If anything, that had made her more eager.

Among their friends, she looked cool and remote as a sea goddess, and as beautiful as one, with droplets of water caressing her succulent body. But she was his to command for the day... well, as long as it was fun for both of them.

Which made her a naughty goddess, but that was the kind he liked best. The kind that made his cock hard again just watching her.

And thanks to the rules he'd set up and she'd agreed to—and the fact that Garth and Alison were pretty damn kinky themselves and liked knowing their guests were having a very good time—he could do something about that hard cock. Right now.

Jack waited until she'd toweled off a bit to make his way to her. He put his arms around her, like any boyfriend stealing a kiss, then whispered in her ear, "Remember what you promised me this morning?"

He actually heard her gulp, and the hint of nervousness gratified him. Serena was usually pretty hard to faze.

She stopped, turned to look up at him with eyes like a doe's— that big, that nervous. "Here?" she whispered. "Now? Is that a good...?"

He shook his head. "Inside."

"Inside? Are you...?" She took a deep breath. "Well, if our host and hostess won't object."

He nuzzled her ear before saying, "Object? They'd be disappointed if no one snuck inside for a quickie."

"In that case...let's go."

He took her hand and led her inside.

The room they ended up in was apparently a game or media room, off the living room and well away from the party going on outdoors.

Once inside, Serena tilted her head up to him, obviously hoping for a kiss, but acknowledging that it had to come on his whim, not hers.

And Jack gave her one.

Oh, he gave her one: a rough kiss, harsh and demanding, his hands pulling at Serena's hair.

Serena moaned deep in her throat, wrapped around him, opened to him as if she'd been waiting for this all day—and maybe she had been. He worked loose the knots holding her top in place as he kissed her, sighing as the slip of damp stretch fabric slithered to the floor and her breasts pressed against him, skin on skin.

He cradled them between his hands, toying at the nipples as he mounded them closer together. His mouth still covered her, drowning out any noises she might be making, but he swore he could taste her aroused, contented sighs.

When he'd dragged her inside, he'd imagined Serena on her knees again, like she had been after breakfast, his hands knotted in her hair, claiming and guiding her, her lips wrapped around him. And god yes, the image made his cock ache with need. Such a sweet mouth on that girl—such a sweet, greedy fuckable mouth. Or maybe his cock nestled between those sweet breasts. No, not nestled—sandwiched, enjoying warm oil and the delicious friction of Serena's flesh, one of those acts that felt purely selfish, just taking his pleasure, an act of dominance that involved no pain, no force, just orgasm for him and teasing enjoyment, but no coming, for his partner.

But now, as his tongue danced in her mouth, another thought was taking over.

Power through pleasure.

Who said the sub always has to be the one on her knees, or that the one on her—or his—knees wasn't getting a kind of power out of being there?

Dumb people, that was who said things like that. The way to a woman's heart, and mind, and soul, was through her pleasure, more often than not—and he was starting to admit to himself that he wanted Serena's heart and mind and soul as well as her body, wanted the whole damn package and not just for steamy, kinky sex.

Okay, definitely for that. But for a whole lot more.

They'd met through a shared interest in BDSM and were just starting to have dates that weren't strictly playdates. Maybe it was time to show her a different side of him—more tender, but still dominant.

Still kissing her, Jack steered Serena to the couch, then broke off the kiss so he could order her to sit down.

Lips swollen from kissing, damp hair in Medusa-like tendrils and tangles, Serena shook her head slightly, less a negation than a clearing, before saying, "Uh, wet bathing suit?" her voice small but not exactly humble—more kiss-dazed, he thought smugly.

"Well, take it off!!"

A lazy grin wakened and spread across her face as she solved the problem. The bathing suit bottom made a satisfying plop as it hit the floor.

He gave her a gentle shove and she sat back on the couch. "Spread your legs," he said, trying to sound authoritative, but to his own ears sounding more eager. Greedy, even.

Was that a bad thing? No, he decided as he gazed at her pink folds, lightly slicked with moisture. Her dark curls were matted from her swim, and it made her look wetter yet, like she'd just been licked into oblivion.

Like she soon would be.

"Wider," he commanded, and without waiting for her to comply, he knelt down between her splayed legs.

"What are you...?"

"Hush." With one hand, he pulled back her outer lips, bringing the inner lips into greater prominence, making her clit stand out like a mini-cock, ready for attention.

"Wait a minute, is this some kind of dom trick? I lie back and enjoy and then get punished for being greedy or selfish or something?" She sounded skeptical, but not particularly alarmed at the prospect of punishment.

Good, she'd figured out that in this relationship, "punishment" was just a code word for an excuse to play harder.

A sharp slap on the inner thigh left a pretty red handprint on her white skin, made her wince one second and smile dizzily the next. "That's for trying too hard to be clever," he said, grinning as he did it, to make clear he wasn't annoyed, just seizing an excuse. "I wish I'd thought of that, actually, but now you'd be onto the trick...so you'd better just lie back and enjoy."

"But...shouldn't I...?"

Jack resisted the urge to snort with laughter, because it really wasn't fair to Serena. She'd figure out for herself, after a little more experience with him, why it was funny. "Serena," he said, forcing his voice into what he thought of as Domspeak, "We've agreed that today you're to do what I tell you to do. What I'm telling you to do is to lie back and enjoy yourself, because right now I feel like tasting you. I like making you scream, Serena. Will you scream for me if I lick you?"

Eyes wide with anticipation now that it had finally sunk in this wasn't a test or a trick, just good old-fashioned oral sex, she smiled and nodded.

He positioned himself and gave a slow, sensuous tonguing

from the juicy opening of her cunt up to her eager clit, savoring the combination of her sweetly smoky juices and overtones of chlorine—usually pool water wasn't on his list of favorite flavors, but blended with essence of Serena it was pretty damn tasty. "There," he said, "not so hard to handle, is it?"

Then he set to work to carry out his threat-or-promise.

Licking delicately at her pouting lips.

Sucking at the juices that flowed from her cunt, wishing he could just stick a straw in and drink them down—she tasted that good to him, that rich and hot and musky.

Nibbling.

Suckling at her protruding clit and inner lips, drawing them into his mouth, working them with lips and tongue until he could sense more juices had flowed, then going back to eagerly lap those up.

(Mustn't stain his friends' couch, after all—he was willing to bet Garth and Alison had already put some interesting stains on it with impromptu sex, but messing up your own upholstery and someone else's were two different things.)

And then Serena couldn't hold back anymore, writhing and mewling; pushing her mound against his probing, exploring mouth; begging for release as he pushed two fingers into her wet cunt and swirled and spiraled around her swollen clit.

Such a hot, sweet, drenched cunt. So tight, and yet so accommodating, opening to his fingers, yet hugging them, squeezing them convulsively as Serena got closer and closer to the edge.

His cock ached to be in there, but dammit, his clever sticking-condoms-in-the-pocket-of-his-shorts trick only worked if he and the shorts were in the same room—and the shorts were in the changing shed by the pool.

"Now," he breathed, talking around her sex, vibrating her clit with his breath. Whether that did it, or the command, or whether his timing was just that good, Serena arched up, shrieked, and clenched at his fingers so hard it seemed to clench his dick at the same instant.

She was shattered by orgasm, but he wasn't done yet. Not by a long shot, not when that quivering pussy tasted so good, not when seeing her lose control like that under his tongue and fingers made him feel like a god.

Serena's eager little body seemed to crave every bit of pleasure he wanted to give it, and she came again and again and still seemed greedy for more.

God, he loved that in a woman.

The dull ache in Jack's cock and balls was getting more distracting, but he was determined to keep going until Serena begged for mercy for her oversensitive clit. Lord, didn't she ever tire? Not that he especially wanted her to—it was just impressive to find someone so responsive, so orgasmic.

So hot and wet and delicious.

Finally, she raised her hand, pounded it on the cushion, muttered, "Enough." When that didn't work, she jerked on his ponytail, trying to raise his head.

Mischievously, he pretended not to notice, giving a few more broad licks, pumping a few more times with his fingers.

"Hey," she protested breathily. "My turn to play!"

He looked up at last.

She pulled him up to her, licked her juices off his chin. Then she wriggled out from under him, encouraged him out of his wet trunks and onto the couch.

She looked so beautiful—so natural and right—kneeling between his legs, her eyes still soft and hazy from coming, her mouth slack and red with desire, her chest and tits mottled and flushed from coming so much.

Jack tried to tell her as much, but Serena's lips descended

onto his cock and he lost the power of human speech.

The room smelled of sex and chlorine, smelled of Serena. His skin was saturated with Serena. He was wrapped up in her, and he loved it.

Her eyes were closed in concentration. Her face was red, scrunched up, distorted by his cock, and that just made it more beautiful from his point of view.

One little hand around the base of his shaft slicked with her own hot juices, the other playing with his balls and with the hot spot he'd pointed out that morning. Her mouth clung and suckled, her tongue swirled, and he wanted to hold on to the moment, to enjoy the sensation a little longer. Then, oh god, she used one finger to gently circle his anus, not entering, just teasing that sensitive opening, and he flashed to the thought of her doing what she was doing while pushing something into him—a finger, a slender dildo, something to complete the cycle.

That did it. Opening his mouth in a silent roar, gripping her shoulders with a death grip, he poured himself into her waiting mouth, into her throat, thinking *Mine, mine, mine!* but unable to make even that much of an attempt at English.

With his last energy, he pulled her up onto the sofa next to him.

Serena roused first, stretched, whispered, "I am *starving!*" She smiled lazily. "Besides, if we're away much longer, it'll give everyone time to make scorecards. I'm sure they heard us outside."

Jack laughed, handed her her bikini bottoms (now unpleasantly clammy, as was his own suit). "Yeah, but was it worth it?"

"Hell, yes!"

ABOUT THE AUTHORS

LISETTE ASHTON is a U.K. author who has published more than two dozen erotic novels and countless short stories. Writing principally for Virgin's Nexus imprint, as well as occasionally writing for Chimera Publishing, her stories have been described by reviewers as "no-holds-barred naughtiness" and "good dirty fun."

JOANNA CHRISTINE is a thirty-something woman living on a little farm in the American South. She holds degrees in many boring things and spent most of the early nineties working on classified projects for the Department of Defense. Now retired from staunch academic pursuits, Joanna tries her hand at novels in various genres under different pseudonyms. This is her first erotica piece.

ADELAIDE CLARK is an author and web editor living in Massachusetts. She mostly writes about rather mundane topics, except when the yearning to write out her dirtiest fantasies hits her. She also penned the story "Feeder" in *She's on Top.*

Bay Area–based **JEN CROSS**, a smut writer and writing workshop facilitator, is a wholehearted believer in the transformative power of smut. Widely anthologized, her writing can most recently be found in *Best Sex Writing 2008, More Five Minute Erotica, Nobody Passes, Best Women's Erotica 2007,* and *Fantasy: Untrue Stories of Lesbian Passion.* Jen's featured at many San Francisco queer-lit venues and she co-facilitates (with Carol Queen!) a monthly Erotic Reading Circle. Want more? Visit www.writingourselveswhole.org.

DREW JAMES DYER is a lapsed scholar who likes to be called "Jim" in bed (likewise in the shower, backseat of his car, etc.). Though he long ago decided that graduate school did not appeal to him as a career path, this doesn't stop him from writing lewd stories about sexy grad students. After writing each such piece, Jim toys ever-so-briefly with the idea of going back for that master's degree after all.

JEREMY EDWARDS is a pseudonymous sort of fellow whose efforts at spinning libido into literature have been widely published online, as well as in anthologies offered by Cleis Press, Xcite Books, and other print publishers. Jeremy's greatest goal in life is to be sexy and witty at the same moment—ideally in lighting that flatters his profile. Readers can drop in on him unannounced (and thereby catch him in his underwear) at http://jerotic.blogspot.com.

EMERALD has been a writer since age seven, though her repertoire did not begin to include erotica until her early twenties. Her

erotic fiction has been published in *Best Women's Erotica 2006,
Erotika: Bedtime Stories, G Is for Games,* and online in GV
Weekly magazine. Currently she resides in suburban Maryland
with her cat and serves as an activist for reproductive justice and
sex workers' rights.

SHANNA GERMAIN doesn't have a favorite sex season,
although if she was tied up and forced to choose, she would
probably pick fall. Her erotic work has appeared in dozens of
anthologies and publications, including *Aqua Erotica 2, Best
American Erotica 2007, Best Lesbian Erotica 2008, Naughty
Spanking Stories A to Z 2,* and *He's on Top.* See more on her
website, www.shannagermain.com.

STAN KENT is a chameleon-hair-colored former nightclub
owning rocket scientist author of hot words and cool stories.
A pleasure-seeking renaissance man who believes oral sex puts
the O in orgasm and is therefore the perfect icebreaker, Stan
uses his worldwide adventures as inspiration for nine unique
and very naughty full-length novels including the *Shoe Leather*
series and dozens of quickie reads on everything from spanking
with shoes to cupcake sex to voyeuristic orgies to techno-rave
group spankings on the dance floor. Never at a loss for something to do with his mouth, Stan has hosted an erotic talk show
night at Hustler Hollywood. The *Los Angeles Times* described
his monthly performances as "combination moderator and lion
tamer." To see samples of his work, his latest hair colors and
travels, visit Stan at www.stankent.com.

SOMMER MARSDEN's work has appeared or is forthcoming
in *Love at First Sting, Whip Me, Tie Me Up, Spank Me, I Is for
Indecent, J Is for Jealousy,* and *L Is for Leather,* among many

others. She also writes regularly for various websites. Please visit her at http://SmutGirl.blogspot or www.freewebs.com/sommer-marsden for more information.

GWEN MASTERS writes everywhere—in the car, in her sleep, even in church. Hundreds of her stories have appeared in dozens of venues, both in print and online, and her novels have been well received by both readers and critics. Gwen, her journalist husband, and their handful of children reside in a historic home near Nashville, Tennessee. To learn more, visit her website, www.gwenmasters.net.

JULIA MOORE is the coauthor of the best-selling book *The Other Rules: Never Wear Panties on a First Date and Other Tips* (Masquerade), a spoof of the tragic dating guide *The Rules*. Her short stories have appeared in *Sweet Life 1* and *2, Naughty Stories from A to Z 1* and *2,* and *Batteries Not Included.*

Canadian eroticist **GISELLE RENARDE** is author of *The Birthday Gift* (Dark Eden Press), short story contributor to *Coming Together: With Pride* (Phaze), and poetry/erotica contributor to the upcoming anthology *The Longest Kiss: Women Write on Oral Sex.* Ms. Renarde lives across from a park with two cats who sleep on her head.

TERESA NOELLE ROBERTS managed to turn her insatiable curiosity about other people's sex lives into a career. Her erotic fiction has appeared in *He's on Top, She's on Top, Caught Looking, Love on the Dark Side, Hide and Seek, Best Women's Erotica 2004, 2005,* and *2007, Succulent: Chocolate Flava 2,* Fishnetmag.com, and many other publications, and she writes erotic romance for Phaze Books. She also writes erotica and erotic romance as half of Sophie Mouette. Sophie's novella "Hidden Treasure" appears in Rachel Kramer Bussel's collection *Bedding Down*.

THOMAS S. ROCHE is the author of hundreds of published erotic stories in many different subgenres and a four-time contributor to the *Best American Erotica* series. He can be found at www.thomasroche.com. "Treatment for a Tongue Job" was inspired by his disappointment on viewing the movie *Cloverfield*—great idea for a monster movie, but not nearly enough cunnilingus.

CRAIG J. SORENSEN's writing has been published in *Tasting Him: Oral Sex Stories* and on the websites Clean Sheets, Oysters & Chocolate, Lucrezia Magazine, and Ruthie's Club.

DONNA GEORGE STOREY is too busy surfing adult sites on the Internet herself to snoop into your history. Her erotic fiction has appeared in many anthologies including *Yes, Sir; Dirty Girls; She's on Top; He's on Top; Best American Erotica 2006; Mammoth Book of Best New Erotica 4–7;* and *Best Women's Erotica 2005–2008*. Her novel, *Amorous Woman*, the story of an American woman's steamy love affair with Japan, was published by Orion in 2007. She currently writes a column "Cooking up a Storey," about delicious sex, well-crafted food, and mind-blowing writing, for the Erotica Readers and Writers Association. Read more of her work at www.DonnaGeorgeStorey.com

Called a "trollop with a laptop" by the *East Bay Express* and a "literary siren" by Good Vibrations, **ALISON TYLER** is naughty and she knows it. Her sultry short stories have appeared in more than seventy-five anthologies including *Sweet Life, Sex at the Office,* and *Glamour Girls.* She is the author of more than twenty-five erotic novels, and the editor of more than forty-five explicit anthologies, including *A Is for Amour, G Is for Games,* and *D Is for Dress-Up* (all from Cleis). Please visit www.alisontyler.com for more information.

RITA WINCHESTER writes her smut from the East Coast. She enjoys neon, dark alleys, and alpha men who tell her what to do. Her work has appeared in *The Mammoth Book of Lesbian Erotica, I Is for Indecent,* and can also be found online at For the Girls, Ruthie's Club, and the Erotic Woman. You can reach Rita at rita_winchester@yahoo.com.

KRISTINA WRIGHT is an award-winning author whose erotic fiction has appeared in over fifty print anthologies, including *Best Women's Erotica, The Mammoth Book of Best New Erotica, Dirty Girls: Erotica for Women,* and *Bedding Down: Winter Erotica.* She loves spending lazy Sunday afternoons in bed, reading, writing, and listening to music. Motown, of course. For more information about Kristina, visit her website www.kristinawright.com.

ABOUT
THE EDITOR

RACHEL KRAMER BUSSEL (www.rachelkramerbussel.com) is an author, editor, blogger, and reading series host. She has edited or coedited over twenty books of erotica, including the companion volume to *Tasting Her, Tasting Him: Oral Sex Stories*, as well as *Spanked: Red-Cheeked Erotica; Naughty Spanking Stories 1* and *2; Yes, Sir; Yes, Ma'am; He's on Top; She's on Top; Caught Looking; Hide and Seek; Crossdressing; Rubber Sex; Sex and Candy; Ultimate Undies; Glamour Girls; Bedding Down;* and the nonfiction collections *Best Sex Writing 2008* and *2009*. Her work has been published in over one hundred anthologies, including *Best American Erotica 2004* and *2006*, Zane's *Succulent: Chocolate Flava 2* and *Purple Panties, Everything You Know About Sex Is Wrong, Single State of the Union*, and *Desire: Women Write About Wanting*. She serves as senior editor at *Penthouse Variations*, and wrote the popular "Lusty Lady" column for the *Village Voice*.

Rachel has written for *AVN, Bust, Cosmopolitan, Curve,*

Fresh Yarn, Gothamist, Huffington Post, Mediabistro, *Newsday,*
New York Post, Penthouse, Playgirl, San Francisco Chron-
icle, Tango, Time Out New York, and *Zink,* among others.
She has been quoted in the *New York Times, USA Today,*
Maxim UK, Glamour UK, GQ Italy, National Post (Canada),
Wysokie Obcasy (Poland), *Seattle Weekly,* and other publi-
cations, and has appeared on "The Martha Stewart Show,"
"Berman and Berman," NY1, and Showtime's "Family Busi-
ness." She has hosted In the Flesh Erotic Reading Series since
October 2005, about which the *New York Times*'s UrbanEye
newsletter said she "welcomes eroticism of all stripes, spots,
and textures." She blogs at lustylady.blogspot.com and
cupcakestakethecake.blogspot.com. Visit the official *Tasting
Her* blog at http://tastingher.wordpress.com.